LOVE
AND
BLARNEY

....

A BALLYBEG ROMANCE

(BOOK 2)

ZARA KEANE

Beaverstone Press LLC
Switzerland

Beaverstone Press

CH-5023 Biberstein

Switzerland

www.beaverstonepress.com

Publisher's Note: This is a work of fiction. Names, characters, places, and incidents are a product of the author's imagination. Locales and public names are sometimes used for atmospheric purposes. Any resemblance to actual people, living or dead, or to businesses, companies, events, institutions, or locales is completely coincidental.

Book Layout © 2014 BookDesignTemplates.com

Ordering Information:

Quantity sales. Special discounts are available on quantity purchases by corporations, associations, and others. For details, contact the "Special Sales Department" at the address above.

Love and Blarney/Zara Keane. -- 1st ed.

ISBN 978-3-906245-05-8

For Adam

CHAPTER ONE

....

BALLYBEG, COUNTY CORK, IRELAND

f Jayme King wanted a metaphor to sum up the mess she'd made of her marriage, finding herself on a flooded Irish road blocked by sheep seemed pretty damned appropriate.

The wipers of her rental car swished back and forth at a frenetic pace. Heavy traffic and even heavier rain had turned what should have been a two-and-a-half-hour drive from Shannon Airport to Ballybeg into a four-hour ordeal. According to the GPS, she'd almost reached her destination... *almost* being the operative word.

Jayme sighed and regarded the ovine roadblock. An elderly man in an olive-green raincoat and tweed cap was herding the sheep. He waved a walking stick at her in a friendly gesture. The sheep inched their way from a pasture on one side of the road to a metal building on the other. If they didn't hurry their furry asses across, she'd lose what little control she had over the standard transmission. Why hadn't she remembered to specify an automatic when she'd made the reservation? But how was she to know the Irish regarded stick shifts as the norm? Remembering to stay on the left side of the road was bad enough. Throwing a third pedal into the equation had turned her impromptu road trip into a nightmare.

She drummed the steering wheel and glanced at the dashboard computer. Nearly nine thirty. If she made it to Ballybeg within the next few minutes, she'd check into her accommodation before hunting down the man she'd traveled over three thousand miles to find.

At the thought of the task ahead, her stomach went into a free fall. What would he say when he saw her? How would he react? And how much would it hurt if he rejected her a second time? Her fingers tensed over the wheel.

Finally the last sheep reached its destination. The farmer doffed his cap at her and disappeared into the metal shelter. Grinding the gears, she shuddered into motion. She didn't want to spend the rest of her life wondering *what if?* She'd already wasted months on tears and regrets. It was time to learn to live again.

***

Ruairí MacCarthy, manager and proprietor of MacCarthy's in Ballybeg, surveyed his domain. The pub had the flair of an Ireland long gone but far from forgotten. The bar was the old-fashioned kind—stained mahogany edged with a tile inlay. He danced his fingertips over the faded wood counter, each scratch a reminder of a previous generation of customers.

Not bad. Not bad at all, especially considering the state of the place when he'd taken control thirteen months ago. Once the renovation was complete, the pub would look similar to when his great-grandfather had hung his shingle over the door in 1927.

He whistled cheerfully, an old tune he couldn't place but couldn't get out of his head. Yeah, life wasn't perfect —not by a long shot—but in comparison to this time last year, things were good.

A fist pounded on the front door.

He paused in the act of polishing a pint glass and frowned. Probably kids messing around. They'd know someone would be in the pub by now, readying it for opening time. He refocused on the task at hand, polishing the glass until it lost its dishwasher dullness and sparkled under the pub's dim light.

This evening, he was knocking off early. And he couldn't bloody wait. The moment the clock struck five, he'd chuck the keys of the kingdom to his sister Marcella and head to Cork City. He smiled to himself and pictured his date. Laura Corrigan was a leggy brunette with generous breasts and a ready smile. But most important, Laura was a laugh. She didn't take herself—or him—too seriously. In short, she was exactly what he needed after the implosion of his marriage. For his first date in years, he was glad it was with someone who was more potential friend than future soul mate. And if their relationship developed into more than friendship, he'd take it one step at a time.

Bang. Bang.

He swore beneath his breath. Could it be one of his sisters? If so, he was in no mood to rush to the door.

"We're not open." His voice was gruff enough to deter whoever was pounding on the pub door before opening time.

Another bang.

For feck's sake. Surely no one in Ballybeg was *that* desperate for a pint. Grumbling, he placed the glass on the counter and tossed his polishing cloth beside it. He shoved up the counter flap and maneuvered his large frame through the gap.

Bang, bang.

"Keep your hair on," he growled. "I'm coming." Through the stained-glass slats in the oak door, he spied a small figure.

Ah, hell.

He loved his sisters, he truly did. But being their go-to person for every disastrous situation they got themselves into was exhausting. What would it be this time? Was Sinéad's renegade boyfriend in jail and in need of bail money? Had Sharon's boss finally come to her senses and fired her? He slid the bolts and braced himself, not to mention his bank account, for the latest episode in the MacCarthy family soap opera.

His chest collided with his visitor's petite form. She took a step back in alarm. He blinked through the heavy rain. She was a small woman and fine-boned, judging by the way her oversized raincoat enveloped her tiny figure.

"Our opening time is the same as every other pub in Ireland," he said, not unkindly. "Ten thirty."

"I'm not here for a drink." One slim hand, wearing a large diamond ring, pushed back the hood to reveal a mane of honey-streaked brown hair and a very familiar heart-shaped face.

His heart rate kicked up a notch when his brain registered who was standing on the doorstep. "Jayme?" His voice was a croak.

"Ruairí." She pronounced his name in the light singsong way of a foreigner who'd tried hard to master which of the many syllables went up in intonation and which went down but hadn't quite gotten it right.

Air exited his lungs in a whoosh. "What are you doing here?"

She tilted her sweet little chin, revealing the cleft he'd once loved to trace with his tongue. "Ask me in and maybe you'll find out."

His feet reacted before his head could process her words. He stood aside and let his estranged wife step over the threshold.

***

Roo-Ree. Jayme let his name roll off her tongue. It tasted like her mom's chocolate-velvet cheesecake.

He'd cut his hair. It now bordered on military short. Gone were his elegant three-piece suits and handmade Italian shoes. He'd replaced them with faded blue jeans and a casual checked shirt, open at the neck. In the two years they'd lived together, Jayme had never known him to wear jeans.

Their eyes clashed in a war of unexpressed emotion and unspoken words. She hadn't seen him in over a year, yet the sight of those broad shoulders and powerful legs still had the power to reduce her to a quivering mass of hormones. Judging by his face, the sight of her had taken his breath away, too—but not, she suspected, in the way she'd hoped.

"What do you want?" His expression morphed from shocked to guarded.

Her mouth was bone-dry. "To talk."

A muscle in his cheek flexed. "You traveled over three thousand miles to talk? Ever heard of the telephone?"

"Your old cell phone number doesn't connect anymore." *Or you've blocked me...* The idea of him cutting her out of his life with such ruthless efficiency sliced into her flesh as sharply as a surgeon's knife.

His gaze hardened. "Why not call the pub? We're in the phone directory."

"I thought it was better to come in person." She clasped her hands to stop them trembling.

He speared her with his hazel eyes, indecision flickering over his handsome features. Eventually he relented. "You'd better get your coat off. You're dripping water all over my clean floor."

She struggled free of the enormous raincoat. When she handed it to him, their fingers brushed, sending a jolt of awareness coursing through her veins. If Ruairí were similarly affected, he hid his reaction well. He examined the raincoat with a frown and raked her body. Heat swept up her cheeks at his scrutiny. Did he like what he saw? She'd chosen her outfit with care: a peach cashmere sweater that complemented her tanned complexion, skinny jeans made by her favorite designer, and gorgeous brushed-leather, high-heeled boots.

"You've lost weight," he said gruffly.

His indifferent reaction to her appearance hurt, even though his assessment was accurate. She'd lost a lot of things over the past year, but her diminished weight was the least of her concerns. "The coat's not mine." She fingered her wet hair. "And its hood was no match for the Irish wind."

He coaxed his lips into a half smile. "Tourist tip: don't bother with an umbrella."

"My landlady beat you to it. The coat's hers, by the way."

The frown returned, and wariness slammed down over his face like iron shutters. "Your landlady? Surely you're not planning on *staying* in Ballybeg?"

His obvious reluctance to be in her presence didn't come as a surprise, but it stung with the force of a million paper cuts. She tilted her chin and met his horrified expression. "I've booked a room at a charming little bed-and-breakfast overlooking the beach."

The line between his brows furrowed. "For how long?"

She gave him a wobbly smile, her bravado in rapid-depletion mode. But she'd come too far to quit and run. "My initial reservation is for a week. Mrs. Keogh says it's no problem if I decide to stay longer because it's off-season."

A muscle in Ruairí's cheek flexed. "It might not be a problem for Mrs. Keogh, but it sure as hell is a problem for me."

The words hit her like a lash. "Please. We need to talk."

His mouth hardened. "We needed to talk a year ago. It's been thirteen months. Why the sudden urgency?"

Actually, it had been thirteen months, three days, and five hours since he'd walked out of their apartment and out of her life. She remembered every second of that awful night down to the tiniest detail. His confession, the fight, and the final horrible moment when he'd told her he was leaving. In the days that followed, she'd thought nothing could have the power to make her feel more wretched.

Boy, had she been wrong.

A wave of grief hit her in the solar plexus, as fresh and as painful as the day her life had truly fallen to pieces. She dragged air into her lungs, shoved the bad memories away, and forced herself to concentrate on the present. "Our divorce will come through in a few weeks."

His eyebrows had always reminded her of a satyr and never more so than when he raised one—as he was doing now. "So? I spent months trying to get in contact with you. You rebuffed my every attempt."

"Please, Ruairí. Don't be this way." She shifted her weight from one sore foot to the other—her beautiful high-heeled boots were *not* suited to the cobbled streets of Ballybeg—and contemplated her strategy. Problem was, she didn't have one. The moment she'd opened the envelope and seen the letter from her lawyer, she'd known what she needed to do. The *how* part of the equation hadn't materialized with the same lightning-bolt clarity.

"You filed for divorce," he said. "You ignored my calls, texts, and e-mails."

"You *left* me." Her voice was wobbly, and unshed tears stung her eyes.

His jaw tensed. "I didn't leave *you*. I left America. I said you could come with me."

"And quit my job from one day to the next? Abandon my whole life?" Her breathing came in short, sharp bursts. "You sprang the news on me the second I walked in the door after a long day at the practice. How did you expect me to react? I thought your parents were dead!"

"I never said they were dead. You assumed—"

"You *let* me assume." The hurt, the pain, the betrayal of that night surged to the surface. "How could you lie to me about something so important? You've met my parents."

"Oh, yeah." His tone was bitter. "And they didn't exactly welcome me with open arms, did they?"

"Seriously? How does their opinion of you count in this argument? They knew you existed, and you knew they existed. You let me think your family was dead. Why would you do that?"

He dropped his gaze to the polished wood floor. "I told you why."

"You told me nothing. All you said was that you were estranged from your family. You hadn't mentioned them to me before *because you didn't think they were relevant.*" Her breath was uneven, her chest rising in time with her indignation. "Yeah, I remember our conversation that night. Every damn word."

The hazel eyes shot up. "Then you remember me telling you it was an emergency. I had to come back to Ireland to sort out a family crisis."

"You said you had to fly *home*—your word, not mine —and stay in Ireland for the foreseeable future." A rebellious tear slid down her cheek, and she rubbed it away with a vicious swipe. "You presented me with a *fait accompli.* How was that an invitation for me to come with you?"

The bar door creaked open. "Jaysus, Ruairí. You've not gone and pissed off your new girlfriend before you've had a chance to shag her?"

The strident voice in its lilting Irish accent made Jayme jump. She whirled around to face the oddest-looking creature she'd ever seen up close and personal. The young woman was a few inches taller than her and sported a shock of spiky peroxide hair dyed green at the tips. She wore an oversized black T-shirt emblazoned with a picture of a deranged-looking priest and the words "Feck Off" capitalized below. Her legs were encased in black leggings. Scuffed lace-up boots completed the ensemble.

The girl was eyeing her with amused disdain. "You can't be serious, bro."

Ruairí grimaced, wearing an expression reminiscent of a condemned prisoner confronted with his executioner. "Marcella, meet Jayme. Jayme, this is my sister."

The other woman quirked a dark eyebrow and extended her hand.

Jayme stared at the beringed fingers with the nails bitten to the quick and hesitated a moment too long before returning the gesture.

Her hesitation was not lost on Marcella. "Charmed, I'm sure," she said in a dry tone, squeezing her hand with enough force to make her wince. "And you are...?"

"Jayme." Perhaps the woman hadn't caught the name when Ruairí had introduced them.

"Jayme..." Marcella prompted with an impatient circular hand gesture.

"Ruairí's wife."

CHAPTER TWO

....

Marcella's sardonic smirk vanished. "His what?" Slack-jawed, she rounded on her brother. "You're married?"

Sweat beaded under the rim of Ruairí's collar. "It's not—"

"You didn't tell your family?" Jayme stared at him, large-eyed.

The hurt in her green orbs sliced him to the core. How could this be happening? Half an hour ago, he'd been fine—not ecstatic over his lot in life, but content. Now his sister—and the woman who'd torn his heart out, stomped on it, and thrown it into the shredder— were both glaring at him with matching expressions of outrage.

His thoughts were racing, his emotions a smorgasbord. He'd known he wasn't over Jayme yet, but he'd been utterly unprepared for the impact of seeing her in the flesh. She wore the signature perfume her grandmother had commissioned from a Parisian perfumer for her twenty-first birthday—floral with a hint of spice. The fragrance sent him hurtling back in time to the heady days of their whirlwind romance and fairy-tale wedding. They'd been ridiculously happy. How could their relationship have gone so wrong, so fast?

"When did this happen?" The force of Marcella's anger jerked him back to the present.

"Three years ago. While I was living in the States."

His sister folded her arms across her colorful T-shirt. "Does Ma know?"

Aw, hell. He squirmed under her razor-sharp glare. "No, Ma doesn't know. The thing is, Jayme and I are getting a divorce."

"*Might* be getting a divorce," Jayme corrected.

His eyebrows shot north. "What do you mean, *might*? You filed for—"

"Enough." She held up a hand. "I'm cold, I'm tired, and I've learned you didn't think our marriage was *relevant* information to share with your family. I'm not in the mood to argue over semantics."

Guilt gnawed at his stomach. Jayme's look of utter devastation slayed him. His eyes wandered down her too-slender frame. Memories of what lay beneath that cashmere sweater surfaced in all their X-rated glory.

He blinked the image into oblivion. He had to think of something to say, preferably fast. Problem was, he hadn't a clue how to handle this situation. "Ten minutes till opening time," he heard himself mumble. "Anyone up for a cuppa?"

His sister put her hands on her hips. "No, I don't want a fecking cup of tea. I want an explanation."

Jayme's startled face regained some of its former composure. "What she said. You owe us answers."

He exhaled sharply. "Right. No tea. How about a coffee?"

"Ruairí!" they exclaimed in unison.

"Fine, fine. I'll talk." He ran a hand through his hair and began to pace. "When I left Ballybeg ten years ago, I cut ties with my family. I had no intention of ever coming back. Frankly, I didn't think they'd miss me."

"Not miss you?" roared Marcella. "You daft eejit. Poor Sharon sobbed herself to sleep for months."

He stopped his pacing. "Months?"

"A few weeks," she conceded. "Okay, a few days. But still. She was upset. We all were."

"I should have told you about Jayme when I got home last year," he said with a sigh. "I was going to but couldn't find the words. It's hard to discuss the stuff that matters, and I was still raw from the breakup. Once the letters from Jayme's lawyer arrived, I figured there was no point."

"Why did you leave Ireland?" Jayme cut in. "I'm assuming you didn't move to America on a whim."

He shifted his focus to her pale face. Hurt lurked in her soft green eyes. He dropped his gaze to her mouth— her sweet Cupid's bow mouth... Okay, mistake. "Our father... isn't an easy man."

His sister snorted. "Which roughly translates to, 'He's an abusive prick with ready fists and a drinking problem.' In other words, he's an Irish cliché. One of the best days of my life was when Ruairí broke his nose."

Jayme's jaw slid lower.

"Marcella, would you mind giving us privacy?" He gave his sister a significant look.

She ignored him. "What you need," she said to her newly discovered sister-in-law, "is an Irish coffee."

Jayme gave a wry smile. "I'm not much of a drinker, particularly not at this hour."

His sister's grin widened. Ruairí's heart sank. What devious plan was she concocting this time? "You should take Jayme out to the farm," she said. "Get Ma to make her one her famous Irish coffees."

He shook his head. "If she drank one of Ma's coffees, she'd be legless."

Jayme frowned in confusion. "I'd be what?"

"Drunk. Very drunk."

"I would like to meet your mother," she said in a quiet voice, "but I might pass on the fortified coffee."

"She's home now." Marcella smirked at him. "Better take her earlier in the day rather than later. Da is in Mallow looking at cattle."

He massaged his temples. Taking his almost ex-wife to meet the clan was the absolute last thing he wanted to do. What would she think of them? What would she say when she saw the state of the farm? "What about the pub?"

"As long as you're back by lunchtime, I'll be grand on my own." She wagged a finger at her brother. "And when you get back, I want to know why you didn't let on you had a wife." She winked at him and headed towards the bar, whistling off-key.

The sweat under his collar began a slow trickle down his spine. If he didn't take Jayme to see his mother before she got wind of his marriage from Marcella, there'd be hell to pay. Having spent the last year trying to rebuild their fragile relationship, he didn't want to lose the connection with his mother. He'd lose *her* soon enough. Shutting his eyes, he shoved the macabre notion to the recesses of his mind. Then he looked straight at the beautiful woman he'd married. She stood ramrod straight, tension oozing from every elegant pore.

"Fine," he said on a sharp exhale. "If you want to meet the rest of my family, let's go. But trust me, if you weren't running to divorce me beforehand, you will be after."

***

Jayme clung to her seatbelt while Ruairí's SUV sloshed through the flooded streets of Ballybeg. The brief glimpse she'd had of the town since her arrival was seen through a haze of mist and rain. Despite the deluge, the bright colors of the buildings contrasted cheerfully with the relentless gray sky.

In other circumstances, she'd have relished a trip to Ireland. One of her great-grandmothers hailed from Donegal, and she'd always had a hankering to visit. Ruairí's reluctance to vacation in his native country had been a disappointment. She'd attributed it to his lack of family. Boy, had she been wrong on that score. She stole a glance at his profile, hard and handsome. "Surely your mom can't be that bad."

He grimaced. "She's bossy, but she's mild-tempered in comparison to my father. Be glad he's gone out." He swerved to avoid a pothole. "*Feck.*"

The rain had increased in the short time Jayme had spent in the pub. The streets of Ballybeg were a few inches deep in water, and the situation was worse once they exited the town proper.

"Gosh," she said, peering through the window, "the flooding is worse than when I drove through an hour ago."

"You drove?" His head swiveled toward the passenger seat. "You remembered to ask for an automatic, right?"

"There was no 'remember' about it," she replied tartly. "How was I to know a standard transmission is the norm in Ireland?"

His laughter reverberated off the worn leather seats. "You mean to tell me that *you* drove a car with gears from Shannon to Ballybeg?"

She folded her arms across her chest and attempted to strike a dignified pose. "Laugh all you want, MacCarthy. I made it, didn't I?"

"So you did. Well done to you." His grin was wide. "I'm more used to seeing you hailing a cab than behind a wheel."

"Frankly, I prefer it that way. The drive was terrifying. Are all Irish roads in lousy condition?"

He laughed. "Many. The roads around Ballybeg were never great. Since the Irish economy collapsed a few years ago, they've been left to go to rack and ruin."

When a car driving on the other side of the road veered into their lane before swerving at the last second, her heart leaped in her chest. "How far is your family's farm?"

"A twenty-minute drive from the town, but it will take us longer in this weather."

"Do you live with them or in Ballybeg? The only address I have for you is the pub."

"I live over the pub. The rooms on the second floor are divided into two apartments. One is mine and the other is Marcella's."

They lapsed into a silence taut with tension. This stranger in jeans and a checked shirt was her husband? Where was the stiff and proper stockbroker she'd married three years ago? Had he ever existed? Had it been a carefully calculated act? The man she'd known would never have been content to run a small bar in Ireland. What had happened to make him do a one-eighty?

"I know very little about you, and you know everything about me." Okay, maybe not *everything*.

He glanced at her sideways before returning his attention to the road. "I didn't lie to you, Jayme. I omitted a few facts."

"A few facts? I'd say you left a lot of stuff out." Anger, confusion, and hurt warred for dominance in her tone of voice with anger emerging the victor. "What part of the tale you spun me was true?"

His brow furrowed but he didn't take his eyes off the road. "Nearly everything. I left Ireland when I got my master's degree. After a brief stint as an intern, I got a job on Wall Street. Seven years and several promotions later, I met you."

She remembered every fruity detail of that cocktail-flavored night. It was her thirtieth birthday, and she'd gone to an exclusive Manhattan nightclub to celebrate. She'd ordered her third—or was it fourth?—cosmopolitan when she'd caught him staring at her across the dance floor.

If his clothes screamed money, his demeanor roared success. She'd held his gaze and flashed him a tipsy come-hither smile. He hadn't hesitated. Within seconds, he'd maneuvered his way through the crowded dance floor and stood before her. The moment she'd heard his Irish accent, each melodious word skittering across her skin in an erotic dance, Jayme had fallen in love.

And she'd assumed he had too. Unshed tears stung her eyes. She blinked them away, dug her French-manicured nails into her palms. "Please, what happened to make you move to another country and never look back?"

He exhaled sharply. "After a massive row with my father, he threw me out and I didn't return. But the row was the catalyst, not the cause. It was more an accumulation of things. Long story short, I was the only one of my siblings to excel in school. Instead of getting a criminal record, I got a university degree—a good one at that. You come from a family where academic prowess is both expected and lauded. I come from one where the ability to pick a lock is considered an essential life skill. How could I tell you about them? Your family is nothing like mine."

"Perhaps not, but why would you think I'd judge you for yours?"

He frowned. "Why wouldn't you? Everyone else does."

"I'm not everyone else. I'm your wife." She clasped her trembling hands in her lap. If only he'd told her the truth. Yes, the image of Ruairí belonging to a family of lawbreakers jarred. No, it didn't fit with the image of the educated, cultured man she'd fallen in love with. But none of that mattered.

"The man you met was a successful stockbroker," he said, a hint of bitterness in his tone. "That's what you saw, that's who you agreed to date, that's who you married."

"Bullshit. I loved you. How could you lie to me? You should have told me the truth about your family before the wedding."

"I was going to tell you. I intended to tell you."

"But?"

His fingers flexed over the steering wheel. "But I got caught up in the whirlwind of our romance. I didn't want our perfect bubble to burst. You have to understand—"

"I don't have to anything. You should have told me. I would have listened."

"Would you?" He turned slightly in his seat, and their eyes met briefly before he returned his gaze to the road. "Come on, Jayme. You'd have realized we weren't right for each other. I know it was selfish, but I couldn't bear the idea of losing you."

"For heaven's sake," she snapped. "You wouldn't have lost me."

He raised one dark eyebrow. "Come on, admit it. You'd have run a mile. Would you have knowingly married a man from my background?"

Her mouth opened on autopilot but she swallowed her protest. Did he have a point? Her parents had made no secret of their disapproved of her husband. They'd raised her to assume she'd marry a man who moved in the same social circles as her family. It was an assumption she'd never thought to question. Until Ruairí, she'd always dated guys her parents would consider son-in-law material. Disregarding his lack of WASP connections was one thing. Would she have turned a blind eye to his unsavory Irish relatives?

"Well?" he prompted. "How would you have reacted if I'd told you?"

"I... don't know," she admitted. "I can honestly say that I don't care now. You're what matters to me, not your background."

They lapsed into a brooding silence as the SUV continued its precarious journey. They'd left the town well behind and were driving past green fields bordered by ancient stone walls. Every now and then, a house dotted the landscape. Some were modern and encompassed every hue and architectural style known to the western world. Others were older: thatched cottages, manor houses, and sprawling bungalows.

Jayme drank in every detail, anxious to steady her racing mind. "They're crooked."

"What?" He slowed when they reached a particularly flooded dip in the road.

"The stone walls. They look like they'll fall down."

"Ah, no," he said with a small laugh. "They're old, but stable."

They turned onto the coast road. The sea was wild. It churned like a whirlpool, foam cresting atop high waves.

"Can you swim in this area?" she asked, pointing toward the water. "The sea looks dangerous."

"Sure you can, once you obey the warning flags. The currents aren't suitable for swimming on some beaches, but others are perfectly safe."

Jayme clasped her fingers on her lap and fiddled with her wedding and engagement rings. She'd lost so much weight since the operation that they now slid up and down her finger with alarming ease. She glanced at Ruairí's large hands at the steering wheel. He was no longer wearing his ring, but the indent where it had once been was still visible. Acid gnawed at her stomach lining. Knowing he considered their marriage to be over shouldn't come as a surprise. And it certainly shouldn't make her soul ache. But it did, and it hurt so damn much.

ZARA KEANE

She returned her attention to the landscape. "How many siblings do you have?"

He slid her a glance. "Three sisters, three brothers."

Her jaw dropped. "Seven kids? Your poor mother."

"Indeed." A smile tugged at his mouth. "Actually, she has eight if we count my father."

He flipped on the indicator, and they turned onto a narrow dirt road. Ramshackle farm buildings were visible to the left, and a small house nestled on a hill to their right.

Ruairí pulled the car to a stop outside the house and killed the engine.

"Your family lives here?" Jayme peered through the car window. "Where did you all sleep? The house doesn't look big enough to accommodate a family of four, let alone nine."

His jaw flexed making her regret her words. "It's not large like your family's house, true, but then most Americans don't live in a mansion."

"I know," she said hurriedly. "It's just—"

The satyr look was back. "Small?"

"I guess." Her cheeks burned. "I didn't mean to offend you."

He drummed his fingers on the steering wheel, his lips forming silent words. He unclicked his seatbelt. "Come on. If you're so keen to meet my family, let's get it over and done with."

26

CHAPTER THREE

....

Ruairí's heart hammered as he guided her to the back of the farmhouse. He was hyperaware of the dilapidated farm buildings and the shabbiness of the main house. Jayme picked her way carefully over the uneven cobblestones in the yard. When they reached the back door, her brow creased in confusion. "Why aren't we using the front door?"

"The front is only for uninvited visitors. We always use the back entrance."

"Why?"

"It's a farm tradition. Avoids filthy boots trekking through the house." He shoved door open and led her through the tiny mudroom toward the kitchen.

Inside Ma was sitting at the battered old kitchen table, a pen behind her ear and a newspaper in her hand. For as long as he could remember, her midmorning ritual involved a mug of steaming tea and the daily crossword. The illness had turned her complexion gray and waxy, but she looked well, all things considered.

His youngest sister, Sharon, sat opposite their mother, bleary-eyed and slouched over a mug of coffee. A dog-eared notebook lay open before her, containing what he hoped were college notes. Da was nowhere to be seen. *Thank feck for small mercies.*

"Ruairí!" Ma leaped to her feet when she spied him in the doorframe, grinning as if he were the prodigal son returned. And in way, he was. "And who's this you've brought with you?"

Jayme lingered in the doorway, uncertainty skittering across her pretty face.

"Come in, love," his mother said. "Don't be shy."

Jayme stepped gingerly down the lopsided step, stumbling when she caught her heel on the uneven edge.

Ruairí caught her arm and righted her. "Are you okay?" He could feel her bones through her voluminous raincoat. She'd always been slight, but this was ridiculous. Her frailty made his protective instincts kick into overdrive. He'd make sure she had a decent meal or two before she flew back to the States.

"I'm fine." She tugged her arm free from his grasp.

Ma stretched out a hand. "I'm Molly MacCarthy."

"Jayme King."

His mother's large hand dwarfed Jayme's. "Are you a friend of Ruairí's?" She put particular emphasis on the word "friend."

"Actually..." Jayme trailed off and looked at him pleadingly.

"Jayme is my wife." He focused on the photograph of the pope that hung menacingly over the drinks cabinet. "But we're getting a divorce."

Ma's hands made an instinctive sign of the cross. "Jesus, Mary, and Joseph. You can't be serious?" She looked from him to Jayme and then back again. "You are serious." She sank back onto her chair. "When did this happen?"

"Did you elope?" Sharon had lost the glazed look and was fully alert.

"No." Jayme bristled and pursed her lips. "We dated for six months and got married three years ago."

"Three years?" Sharon roared with laughter. "You are a dark horse, brother."

Ruairí wished the cracked linoleum floor would swallow him whole.

"Why didn't you tell us?" Ma demanded. "We're your family. We had a right to know."

"I'm telling you now, aren't I?" he said, squirming under their scrutiny.

"And what's this nonsense about a divorce?" His mother's fingers fluttered to the crucifix around her neck. "MacCarthys don't get divorced. We're like swans. We mate for life."

A fleeting image of his father's bullish face floated before him. "In some cases, we should rethink that stance."

Ma's crestfallen expression cut him to the quick. "I don't understand why you didn't tell us. You've been home a year."

"He's ashamed of us." Sharon's words held no rancor, merely resigned acceptance of the status quo. "That's why he left Ballybeg in the first place. And by the look of the wife, she's too fancy for the likes of us."

"Don't judge me before we've been introduced," Jayme said coolly. "Which of the six siblings-in-law I never knew I had are you?"

His little sister's lips quivered with reluctant amusement. "I'm Sharon."

"I'm delighted to meet you." Jayme gestured at a free chair. "May I join you?"

"Of course." Ma was rapidly recovering her composure. "Make yourself at home. Can I tempt you with an Irish coffee? I think I need one."

Jayme hesitated a fraction of a second before nodding. "All right. I guess I am on vacation."

"Great stuff." Ma leaped to her feet. "Will *you* join us?"

"I'm driving," he said. "Should you be drinking, Ma? The doctor—"

"I'm dying, not dead. Let me live a little while I still can, eh? A drop of whiskey won't make any difference to my prospects at this stage."

Jayme sat poleaxed at the table, her normally mobile hands frozen in her lap. "You're sick?"

"Did he not tell you?" Ma pulled a bottle of whiskey from the drinks cabinet and a carton of cream from the fridge. "Ah, why am I even asking? Of course he didn't. Sure, that's why he came back to Ireland."

Jayme's gaze bore into him. "He mentioned a family emergency, but he didn't elaborate."

"Men, eh? Typical." Ma whipped the cream to a fluffy froth. Ruairí brewed the coffee. He poured a cup for himself and whisked it away before his mother could attack it with the whiskey bottle.

"Go easy on the whiskey in Jayme's, will you?" he said as he eased himself onto one of the hard kitchen chairs. "She's not used to your idea of a small drop."

Jayme gave a small smile. "With the morning I'm having, I say bring it on."

"That's the spirit," Ma said. "I've a feeling we'll get on grand."

"May I ask what's wrong with you?"

"Cancer, love. I had a bout a few years back, and it looks like this time I won't beat it."

"Which treatments have you had?" He could visualize her brain cataloging various options with computerlike efficiency. "With all the new drugs available these days —"

Ma set a mug of Irish coffee before Jayme and reclaimed her seat. "No more chemo. No more radiation. I'm done with all of that. What I've got isn't going away, no matter what fancy drugs they pump into my system. Now enough about my health." She raised her mug to them. "*Sláinte.*"

"*Sláinte.*" The word sounded hesitant on Jayme's tongue.

His mother took a sip of her fortified coffee. "What do you do for a living, Jayme?"

"I'm a doctor. A pediatrician to be exact."

"Ah. That explains the medical questions. Well, our Ruairí was always the smartest of the bunch. I'm not surprised he found a smart woman to marry."

Jayme blushed, and her gaze met his for the briefest of seconds.

"It's a great comfort to me to know the pub is in good hands," his mother continued. "If it was left to Colm to run—that's my husband—it would be bankrupt in weeks. The pub was always my domain."

Ruairí shifted uncomfortably on his chair. Jayme was studiously not looking in his direction, but he was cognizant of every breath she took.

"How long are you staying in Ballybeg?" Sharon asked, shoving a triangle of toast into her red-rimmed mouth.

"I've taken a week off work."

"You should try and see a bit of the place while you're here," Sharon said. "The weather's supposed to improve over the weekend."

Ma pointed to a picture on the calendar by the door. "Take her to Blarney Castle. Let her see where our ancestors lived."

Jayme perked up visibly. "Is that where the Blarney Stone is kept?"

"It is indeed. Get him to take you."

Ruairí shot his mother a warning look. "I have to work, Ma."

"I'll cover for you on Monday," Sharon said with deceptive innocence.

He eyed her with suspicion. "Don't you have lectures?"

She shrugged. "I can always get the notes from another student."

"I wouldn't like to inconvenience you," Jayme said quickly.

"It's no bother." Sharon wiped crumbs from her chin and shot her brother a wicked look. "Yeah, you should definitely get him to show you around Cork. No point in coming all this way and not doing something touristy."

Ruairí swallowed a sigh. His mother and sister were lousy liars and unsubtle matchmakers. He watched Jayme's hopeful face. She'd always wanted to travel, and she'd often talked about coming to Ireland. When they'd visited Mexico on their honeymoon, they'd vowed to vacation at least once a year. Thanks to their busy work schedules, it hadn't happened. He could hardly deprive her of the opportunity to see a bit of Ireland now that she was here. "All right. I'll take you to see a few tourist spots."

She glowed with happiness. "Really?"

"Really. But in the meantime, we'd better go." He rose and scraped his chair across the floor.

"So soon? But you only got here." Ma's look of disappointment needled his already guilty conscience.

"I told Marcella I'd be back at the pub before the lunchtime rush."

"I'd love to come back to see you before I leave, Mrs. MacCarthy," Jayme said. "If that's okay."

Ma beamed. "Of course it's okay. And please call me Molly. You're family, after all."

They'd barely reached the mudroom when the back door swung open. In marched his little brother, Shea.

"Thank feck you're here," Shea said when he spotted Ruairí. "Come and help me. One of the cows is after bolting."

"In this weather?"

Shea grimaced. "Exactly. It's Daisy, too."

"Feck." Daisy was pregnant and known to be a bit contrary of late. "I'll put on my wellies."

"Let me help," Jayme said, reaching for his arm. A familiar frisson of awareness passed between them. Having her in close proximity was rapidly shredding every vestige of self-control he possessed.

He glanced at her feet. "In those shoes? I think not. And I doubt any of us has wellies small enough to fit you."

"Never mind my boots. I'm happy to assist."

"Let her," Shea said bluntly. "I need all the help I can get. And if she and Sharon come, Ma can stay in out of the rain."

Jayme grabbed her raincoat from the coat stand. "Let's go."

....

CHAPTER FOUR

"What do you know know about cows?" Jayme wiped rain from her nose and looked at her handsome companion. He was regarding her with a cynical half-smile. "I know that they moo."

He laughed. "If you want to help us look for Daisy, that's fine. But don't go anywhere near her if you see her. She's pregnant and irascible. Give one of us a shout, and we'll deal with her."

They'd parted ways with Shea and Sharon at the cowshed. Thankfully, the rain had dwindled to drizzle, but the ground was wet and slick with mud. She was grateful to have Ruairí at her side, deftly guiding them past the deepest of the puddles.

"I'm glad your family's farm is on higher ground than the road. Otherwise, we'd have to swim."

He grinned a slow, teasing smile that warmed her from the top of her scalp down to her ill-clad toes. "How are your feet holding up? Those boots don't look waterproof."

"My feet are a little damp," she admitted, "but I'll cope."

He led her toward lush green fields separated by the old-fashioned stone walls she'd noticed on their drive. With each step, her boots sank deeper into the mud. "How long does your mother have to live?"

His face darkened at the question. "Initially, the doctors gave her six months. A year later, she's still with us. She's doing reasonably well at the moment, but they warned us her condition could take a turn for the worse at any moment."

On instinct, she slipped her small hand into his large one. He didn't resist. "Why didn't you tell me your mother was sick?"

He turned his attention to the pasture. "I don't know. The night I left, we were too busy fighting. To be honest, I half suspected it was a scheme cooked up by her and my sisters to get me to come home and reconcile with my father. Whatever Marcella says, it wasn't my decision to cut ties with my entire family. When I left, my father forbade my mother to contact me."

"And she obeyed?" She entwined her fingers with his, watched his Adam's apple bob.

"Yeah." He blinked a few times, failing to conceal the moisture in his eyes. "But it was a long time ago. I got over it and lived my life."

"And met me."

"And met you."

They lapsed into silence. The tension of earlier had eased, but the connection between them remained tenuous. "Was it your mother who called you last year? The night we fought?"

He inclined his head a fraction. "She called me at work, out of the blue. I thought it was some sort of sick joke at first, but Ma was direct. Said the doctors didn't give her long to live and that both the pub and the farm were in the red. Shea had taken over the running of the farm, and she needed someone to take charge of the pub before Da ran it into the ground."

"Why didn't she ask Marcella?"

"Marcella has no head for business and even less interest. She likes chatting with the customers when she's in the mood. However, her real passion lies in the kitchen. She's responsible for all our hot food."

"What about your other brothers and sisters?"

"Sinéad and her boyfriend have six-month-old twins —with all that that implies. Sharon is still at university. She has a part-time job at the local bookstore to tide her over financially. While she works the odd shift at the pub if we're stuck, I don't want her chucking in her studies to work there full-time. Shea, as I said, is responsible for the farm. Our youngest brother, Mikey, helps him out."

"What about your father?" she asked, then paused. "Wait... isn't a brother missing from that list? You said you had three, right?"

"Yeah. Colm Senior—our father—and Colm Junior have more in common than their names. Let's just say they're both well known to the local police and have done more than one stint in prison. To put it bluntly, Colm Junior is currently incarcerated."

She tried to wrap her mind around the idea of staid, sensible Ruairí having a brother in jail. "I see."

"No, you don't." His laugh was bitter. "How can you? My family is a wild bunch. They never had an opinion they didn't express. I left Ireland for America because I wanted a fresh start. To be someplace where no one knew my background or me. For a while, I lived the dream. And then my mother called, and my past and present collided."

And the past had won. The hollow sensation in the pit of her stomach fed into her self-doubts. "Your mother said she was responsible for the pub until she got sick, hence the crisis."

Ruairí nodded. "My father inherited the pub from his father. For a few years, he ran it with my Uncle Buck. When it became apparent Da and Buck were drinking more than the customers, Ma stepped in and took over. For years, the pub was her domain."

"Until she got sick," Jayme finished for him.

"Yes. Until she got sick." He flexed his fingers. "With Ma out of commission, the place was going downhill fast. Colm Junior and a prison pal of his took over the day-to-day running of the place. The results were predictable. Within a couple of months, the pub had been raided twice. The second raid bore fruit—Colm and his pal were arrested for possession with intent to supply and sent down."

Jayme whistled. "Wow. And then you arrived to save the day."

"Yeah." He halted, jerking his gaze away from the path ahead. He squeezed her hand. "I'm so sorry, Jayme. I should have told you all of this last year. When I first came over, I had no intention of staying in Ireland. When I saw the state of the pub—not to mention the state of my family—I couldn't up and leave."

She swallowed past the razor blades in her throat. "You up and left me."

"Sweetheart—"

"Did you really think I was so superficial that I'd reject you if I knew your dad and brother were jailbirds? Or that I'd object to you helping your sick mother? For heaven's sake, I'm a doctor. I'm all too familiar with cancer and its ramifications."

"Jayme, your mom is one of the most renowned pediatricians in New York, and your dad is the state attorney general."

"So? I fell in love with *you*, not your family. *You're* not a jailbird. What does my background have to do with you not telling me your mom was sick?"

"Nothing. You're absolutely right. I should have told you straight out.

Out of the corner of her eye, she caught a glimpse of black and white. Slipping her hand free of his grasp, she ran to the fence to take a closer look. "Ruairí, is that your missing cow?"

He fished binoculars from his coat pocket and peered through them. "That's Daisy, all right." He flipped open his phone and hit a number on the display. "Shea? We've got her. She's down in the south meadow by the water trough."

The cow was immobile, possibly mired in mud. "What do we do?" Jayme craned her neck to get a better view.

"*You* do nothing. Let me and Shea deal with her."

A few minutes later, Shea ran down the track to join them, spraying mud with every step. "Damn," he said, staring through the binoculars. "She's stuck, but not too deep, thank feck."

Ruairí turned to her, his mouth a hard line, and worry lines etched by the corners of his eyes. "Wait here. We'll try to get her out."

Twenty excruciating minutes later, Ruairí and Shea had part coaxed, part dragged a very reluctant Daisy back to the cowshed.

Sharon was waiting for them by Daisy's stall. She fussed over the cow upon her arrival, cooing to her as though she were a baby. Within a few minutes, Daisy had been rubbed down, covered in a warm blanket, and supplied with food and water.

Outside the shabby cowshed, the gray sky showed cracks of blue. Jayme glanced around. The farmyard was small and consisted of four buildings in various stages of collapse. Snorting was audible from one of the smaller buildings. She wandered over to investigate.

The heel of one of her boots caught between the cobblestones. One second, she was upright. The next, she was nose first in the mud. Nose first in particularly foul-smelling mud... "Oh, fff—"

Twenty-four hours ago, she'd been dining on sushi in one of Manhattan's most exclusive restaurants. Today, she was ass over heels in an Irish farmyard, her face stuck in a pile of cow excrement. How had this happened to her? Oh, yeah... a brush with death and a rush of blood to the head. In short, she'd lost what vestiges of sanity she still possessed.

"Cow shite," said a thunderous voice from above.

Jayme pushed herself up to her elbows and sneezed.

A wild-haired man loomed over her, brandishing a walking stick. "Who the hell are you? And what the fuck are you doing on my farm?"

Ruairí emerged from the cowshed, Shea at his heels. "Back off, Da. Aren't you supposed to be in Mallow?"

The man with the stick glared at them. "The roads were flooded. I had to turn back." He gestured at Jayme with his walking stick. "I don't like trespassers on my property."

"She's not a trespasser. She's with me." Grabbing her arm, Ruairí hauled her to her feet in one fluid movement. He fished in his coat pocket and produced a clean tissue. "For your face." She noted both his protective stance toward her and the belligerent look he was directing at his father.

The older man spat on the ground. "If she's with you, take her away. I don't want any friend of yours on my farm. And take yourself away while you're at it."

"Steady on. Jayme's my guest."

"On *my* farm. You've stolen my pub. You needn't think you'll get the farm as well."

Ruairí rolled his eyes. "I bought the pub off you and Ma—lock, stock, and Guinness barrel. And I paid well over the going rate."

Colm Senior's nostrils flared, and his bloodshot eyes bulged. "Get off my land, the pair of you."

Ruairí's grip on her shoulders tightened. "Come on. Let's get you home for a shower."

"Bye, Jayme," Sharon said from the entrance to the cowshed. "Nice to meet you."

"And you." Jayme swallowed something and winced at the taste.

Shea nodded to her but remained silent, his wary eyes trained on his father.

When they reached the car, she turned to Ruairí. "Aren't you going to tell your mother that Daisy is safe?"

He shook his head. "Better get going before my father comes up to the house. We can call in on her another day."

Jayme slid into the passenger seat, still trembling with shock and fury. "What a horrible man."

He gave a bitter laugh and started the ignition. "Believe it or not, you got him on a good day."

"Seriously? How did you put up with such abuse?"

The SUV bumped back down the path and turned onto the main road.

He shrugged. "As crazy as it sounds, we were used to him when we were kids. As I grew up, I started to stand up for my mother, but it was usually a bad idea. That's why I left. I couldn't stand it any longer. If we'd all stood up to him, then maybe we could have gotten him to leave us alone. But I was the only one crazy enough to take him on. When the others refused to intervene, I'd had enough."

On the dashboard, his phone vibrated. He switched it to loudspeaker. Marcella's cheery tones crackled down the line. "You're not going to believe this, but I've gone and got an interview for that cookery course I was telling you about. You know, the one in Cork City."

"Yes." Ruairí drew out the word in a wary manner.

"It's the day after tomorrow. I'm really sorry, bro, but I'll have to take a couple of days off work. I need tomorrow to get my portfolio together. The interview is the day after."

"Is this true or is it one of your matchmaking schemes?"

"What? Oh, the line is breaking up." Something that sounded like aluminum foil echoed down the line. "Talk when you get back to the pub, 'kay? You'll need to find someone to cover for me. Maybe Jayme can help if she's around."

The line went dead.

"Bloody Marcella," he said in annoyance. "I'll bet Ma called her. She's about as subtle as a boulder."

Not subtle, thought Jayme, but her newly discovered sister-in-law might have provided her with the perfect opportunity to spend time with Ruairí. "Do you think she was serious? What's this cookery course she mentioned?"

"It's at a fairly prestigious school. She's wanted to take one of their courses for years, but they're expensive and she didn't have the resume to get in. She's spent the last few years building her portfolio and saving to apply for the course. And now it seems she has an interview."

"But that's fantastic news," Jayme said, smiling. "Isn't it?"

"Fantastic news for her. Not so much for me. If she needs two days off work at such short notice, I'm going to be scrambling to find someone to fill in."

"So let me help you."

He stared at her as if she'd sprouted horns. "What do you know about serving in a pub? Or preparing hot meals en masse?"

"How hard can it be to figure out? Come on. Give me a chance to prove to you I'm not the pampered princess you seem to think I am. If you're worried about the hot food aspect, we can change the menu to soup and sandwiches for a couple of days."

He scratched his chin. "I'd have to check the legalities of allowing you to work in the pub. You don't have a work permit."

"You won't be paying me. I'll be your wife, helping you out behind the bar. Who'll object to that?"

Uncertainty flickered across his face.

"Come on, Ruairí. Please."

He sighed. "Fine. We can try it for a couple of days. Just until Marcella gets back."

She beamed at him. On impulse, she leaned over and planted a kiss on his cheek, noting the stubble teasing her lips.

He shook his head. "How do you manage it? You're filthy, you stink, and yet you still exude sex appeal."

His words warmed her from her soaked toes to her damp hair. "You won't regret it, Ruairí. I promise."

CHAPTER FIVE

···

"Slow down." Ruairí observed the action closely. "A decent pint of stout needs time to settle." It was his new assistant's first day on the job. She'd breezed in an hour before opening time, impeccably groomed and wafting her signature scent. He suppressed a smile. Her optimism was sure to evaporate as soon as she encountered the pub's regular customers.

"Ah, no. Not like that." He moved behind Jayme and put his hands over hers. They were smooth and soft. "Hold the pint glass in your right hand at a forty-five-degree angle. Yeah, that's better. Then ease the tap handle all the way down until it's horizontal."

"Like this?" She glanced up at him, uncertainty clouding her bright green eyes.

"Yeah, that's good. Whoa, stop there." He shoved the tap handle up. "Now let the surge settle."

She wrinkled her pretty little nose in concentration. "For how long?"

"Two minutes, give or take." Her tight little arse was nestled right about groin level. He exhaled sharply and shifted position.

"And once it's settled?"

"Then you repeat the process until the glass is full."

"Wow." She examined the quarter-full glass. "Does it really take so long to pull a pint of Guinness?"

"If you want to do it right, yes. And in my pub, we do it right." Many modern barmen rushed the job, anxious to serve the next customer. Not Ruairí. He took pride in MacCarthy's being known for the quality of its pints. Satisfied customers were his reward.

The door of the pub was thrown open in a flurry of wind and rain. John-Joe Fitzgerald limped inside. His Elvis quiff was windblown, and his stained sleeveless vest offered scant protection against the heavy rain. John-Joe was utterly unperturbed by his damp and disheveled state. He dragged his bad leg across the room and hauled himself up on his favorite barstool. "Morning, Ruairí."

All of Jayme's prep school manners deserted her. She gaped at the new arrival in obvious horror.

"Morning, John-Joe," Ruairí said. "What can I do you for?"

"Ah, I'll have the usual." The older man raked Jayme with greedy eyes, his gaze lingering on her breasts. "Who's the new barmaid?"

"This is Jayme." There was a hard edge to Ruairí's voice. "My wife."

The man's beady eyes widened a fraction. "You have a wife?"

"He does," Jayme said, inching closer to his side. "Are you a regular customer?"

John-Joe inclined his thick neck. "I've been sitting on this here barstool for four decades and counting."

She whistled. "That's quite a while."

John-Joe patted his impressive beer belly. "I've invested a lot of time and money in my physique."

"What did you do to your leg?" Ruairí indicated the injured limb, now propped up on a neighboring barstool.

"Ah, you know how it is." John-Joe displayed a set of incongruously white teeth. "I'm getting to be a bit old to do the old pelvic thrusts on stage."

"Pelvic thrusts?" Jayme looked at both men for an explanation.

"John-Joe is Ballybeg's resident Elvis impersonator," Ruairí said, deadpan.

"I'm a Swimming Elvis," the older man said indignantly. "I'm not any old impersonator. People get something extra special at my shows."

Jayme was struggling to keep a straight face. "What does a Swimming Elvis do?"

"I strip out of my King suit down to my swimming shorts. The punters love it."

Ruairí chuckled at her aghast expression. "Ballybeg doesn't need the Chippendales when we have John-Joe." He grabbed the pint Jayme had prepared and shoved it toward John-Joe. "Here you are. You have the honor of drinking Jayme's very first pint of stout."

John-Joe took a cautious sip, and then licked the foam from his lips. "Not bad. Not bad at all."

She beamed. "Ruairí's a good teacher."

"So what do you do when you're not working as a barmaid? You look a bit posh to be behind a bar."

"I'm a pediatrician at a private practice in Manhattan."

"A doctor, eh? We're short of those in Ireland. Always having to import people." John-Joe leaned closer. "I'm never sure if half of them understand me."

Given Jayme's look of bemusement, Ruairí guessed she was having problems following the man's thick accent. He gave her a gentle nudge. "Can I finish giving you a tour of the place before the lunchtime rush?" In the hour before opening, he'd given her a quick glimpse of the disco and the smoker's den that were located behind the pub's main building, but most of their time had been spent showing her how to mix drinks, pour pints, and work the fickle cash register.

"Sure," she said, fiddling with a loose strand of hair.

He shoved up the counter flap and gestured for her to walk through. "The main taproom is where we serve most of our customers Sunday through Thursday. We also have a lounge through here with a pool table and a dartboard. We took out the separating doors years ago and serve the lounge customers directly at the main bar."

She surveyed the lounge and nodded. "Do you wait on the customers, or is it self-service only?"

"We have extra staff on Fridays and Saturdays. Then people have the option of being served at the bar or directly at their tables." He led her across to a half-concealed room down a short flight of steps. "And this here is the snug."

Her brow creased in confusion. "The what?"

He gave a bark of laughter. "The snug."

She peered into the small room. Ruairí followed her gaze, drinking in the sight of plush chairs and sofas. On his friend Gavin's advice, he hadn't followed the modern trend of ripping out the snug to enlarge the main bar area. Instead, he'd wallpapered it with vintage newspaper and restored the brass bell to its former sheen. A glow of pride warmed his stomach. The place was looking good.

"It's adorable." Jayme ran her fingers over a soft velvet sofa. "Why do you call this room a snug?"

"In the old days, it was a private room in the pub where people not welcome in the taproom could enjoy a drink. Women, children, priests, and the like. They'd ring this bell"—he indicated the brass button on the wall —"and someone would come and take their order. We still use the bell on Fridays and Saturdays, but the snug is part of the regular bar now. The drinks cost the same as anywhere else in the pub."

"I'd imagine these tables are coveted." Her fingertips danced over the bell.

How could he be envious of an inanimate object? "Yeah. All the furniture is new. We're in the middle of a renovation at the moment, although most of it's already finished. We're waiting to do the lounge until Gavin, my architect, gets back from Australia."

"It looks really nice."

The sight of her smile triggered a familiar fluttering sensation in his stomach. "I know it's not the sort of bar you're used to."

"We're not in Manhattan," she said with a laugh. "I don't expect places to be the same when I travel."

Their eyes met, sparking a frisson of electricity. God, how he'd missed her. He'd regretted his decision to leave the moment he'd boarded the plane to Ireland. They'd barely landed when he'd called to apologize, but she'd made it clear she needed time to think. Over the next few months, he'd left numerous messages on her voice mail and sent countless e-mails. And the only response he'd received were the letters sent by her divorce attorney. He stepped closer and drew her deeper into the snug, away from John-Joe's curious eyes. "Why are you here, Jayme? What prompted you to change your mind?"

Her mouth moved, but no sound came out. When she finally spoke, her voice wobbled with emotion. "I wanted to see you. I needed to know if our marriage was truly beyond salvation. If I'd waited any longer, the divorce would have been finalized."

They stood toe-to-toe, close enough to kiss. For the first time in his adult life, he regretted that divorce in America was so much quicker than in Ireland. He leaned down and ran his hands through her gorgeous hair. "Jayme, I—"

"Ruairí," John-Joe yelled from the main room, "you've got another customer."

She jerked back, out of his grasp. They were both breathing heavily.

"I'd better—" He gestured toward the taproom.

"Sure." She smoothed her already-perfect hair. "You can finish the tour afterward."

Back in the main room, the pub's other stalwart regular customer—his uncle Buck—sat beside John-Joe. What Buck lacked in hair, he did not make up for in intelligence, but Ruairí was fond of him all the same. "What can I get you?"

"Ah, throw me a packet of those dry-roasted peanuts, would you? And you might as well pull me a pint of stout to go with them."

"Coming right up."

Buck's habit of ordering a packet of crisps or peanuts and adding his drink as if it were an afterthought never failed to amuse him. Buck was his father's brother. As good-natured as Colm was mean, he was rarely sober and had a tendency to fall for every get-rich-quick scheme that stumbled across his path.

"Molly tells me you've taken a bride," Buck said when Ruairí slid a pint in front of him.

"Not exactly." His eyes flickered toward Jayme. "We got married three years ago." *And we're in the process of getting a divorce...* The words stuck in his throat.

"Aye?" Buck peered myopically at Jayme. "She's a looker all right."

"Yes, she is," he said, watching her pour herself a glass of water. He shouldn't be enjoying having her around as much as he was. She'd be gone by the end of next week. But she was a ray of sunshine in his otherwise mundane existence. He didn't miss the rat race or the cutthroat mentality of Wall Street. He didn't miss his phony friends—only a couple had bothered to keep in touch once it became clear that he intended to stay in Ireland and run the pub.

But he missed Jayme. Every damn day. He'd been a fool to think he was moving on, starting to get over her. One glance at her sweet face and delicate curves, and he'd been a goner.

She caught him looking at her and raised a slim eyebrow. "What are you staring at? Am I doing something wrong?"

"Not at all. You're perfect."

She laughed. "I doubt that, but I am trying."

He caught her hand and pulled her out of earshot. "Jayme?"

"Yes?"

"Thanks for coming over to Ireland." His voice cracked with emotion. "You were right to force us to talk in person. It's too easy to pretend at a distance. But we are going to have to sit down and decide... how to proceed."

She nodded and entwined her fingers with his. She rubbed the indent where his wedding ring had been. "What did you do with your wedding band?"

Hurt lurked in those beautiful eyes. He smiled and fished a chain out of his shirt. "I wear it over my heart."

She laughed. "You liar! You always hated that ring."

"No, I don't hate it. I certainly don't hate what it symbolizes." He unfurled his hand and showed her the indent. Small scales of hard skin were still visible. "See this? The ring gave me a rash and it's only starting to heal now, months after I stopped wearing it."

"A rash?" She examined his finger closely. His pulse quickened at her touch, sending tiny jolts of electricity coursing through his veins. "Do you think you're allergic to platinum?"

"Is that possible? I've heard of nickel allergies, but I thought platinum was safe."

Jayme shook her head. "Platinum allergies are rare, but they certainly exist. Why didn't you tell me the ring was bothering you?"

Their eyes locked. "I didn't want to hurt your feelings. You chose our wedding bands."

"Yeah, but I don't want you wearing a ring that makes you itch. We could have traded yours in for one made from a different metal."

"But then our rings wouldn't match."

"So? As long as you're comfortable, that's all that I care about."

They stared at one another in silence. Would it have been that simple? Why hadn't he told her the ring was bothering him instead of adding it to the mountain of things they simply didn't discuss? Jayme was sweet and caring and a great listener. So why had he felt it necessary to bottle up his emotions and hide his feelings from her? Force of habit? Growing up with Colm MacCarthy as a father, he'd mastered the art of affecting a neutral mask from an early age.

The sound of John-Joe hacking up phlegm broke their connection. She let go of his hand and stepped back, shoving a stray lock of honey-streaked hair behind one ear. "I guess I'd better get a start on lunch."

"It won't be too much for you?"

"As long as we stick to the plan of serving soup and sandwiches instead of the full menu, I'll manage. Even my limited culinary skills extend to sandwiches."

On impulse, he grabbed her hand. "Want me to show you around Ballybeg this evening? I was going to walk you back to your bed-and-breakfast in any case. Might as well combine the two."

Her heart-shaped face broke into a smile. "I'd love that. Thank you."

Ruairí released her, and she disappeared into the kitchen, leaving him with a still-outstretched hand and a hollow sensation in his stomach. He stared at the space she'd occupied. Twenty-four hours ago, he'd been fooling himself that he was content with his lot, despite the gaping hole left by Jayme's absence. Today, he had no idea how he was going to cope when she left him for good and returned to her reality on the other side of the Atlantic.

CHAPTER SIX

....

A t six o'clock that evening, Ruairí's youngest sister, Sharon, strutted into the pub. Under her short denim jacket, she wore a tight sequined top cut so low that even Jayme was riveted by her cleavage.

Ruairí tossed Jayme her coat. "Now Sharon's here, we can go for our walk." "Sounds great," she murmured. The sight of the girl's hair was distracting. Had it been that bouffant the previous day? Or that blond?

"Extensions." The younger woman patted the peroxide bird's nest with pride. "Do you like them?"

"I..." she stammered. "Well..."

Ruairí emerged from behind the bar and examined his sister's hair. "They look like shite."

Sharon was unperturbed by her brother's blunt assessment. "Sure, what do you know about women's fashions?" She shrugged off her jacket and slipped behind the bar.

Jayme pulled on her coat and reached for her purse. The pub was quiet apart from Buck and John-Joe and two men in police uniforms who were seated at a corner table. "Will you be okay on your own? I'm not sure I'd want to run a bar at night by myself."

The girl's scarlet-rimmed mouth curved into a smile. "I'll be grand. Sure, don't I have the local police to come to my rescue if necessary?" She jerked a thumb at the cops' table. "Do you hear that, Brian Glenn? You're responsible for maintaining law and order in this establishment."

The younger of the policemen blushed a fiery red. "The only risk to the peace I see is *you*, Ms. MacCarthy."

Sharon roared with laughter. When she'd calmed down, she turned to Jayme. "Are you two off on a date?"

"Your brother is giving me a tour of the town."

"In the dark?" The girl flashed a cheeky grin. "Sounds romantic."

"Come on." Ruairí placed a hand on Jayme's shoulder and nudged her into motion.

"Enjoy yourselves," Sharon called after them. "Don't worry about a thing. The pub will still be standing come morning."

Outside, Jayme pulled her coat tight across her chest to ward off the damp night air. She observed her surroundings. Despite the dark sky, the town was well illuminated by inside lights and street lamps.

"I hope you don't mind having a tour in the dark." His deep voice was hesitant.

"Not at all. At least it's not raining."

They strolled down the cobblestoned lane. The pub was located on a small side street off the main square. Each building in the center of Ballybeg was painted a different color. The forest green facade of MacCarthy's was tame in comparison to some of its brightly colored neighbors. The rainbow effect should have looked garish. Instead, it lent the town a cheerful appearance in spite of the inclement weather.

When they came to the square, she pointed to a stone edifice of a tall man wearing a twenties-style suit. "Who's the statue?"

"That's Michael Collins. He was one of the leaders during Ireland's fight for independence. He grew up not far from here and was killed in Cork during the Irish Civil War."

They crossed the square and took another side street. She was painfully aware of every slippery cobblestoned step. Reaching the smooth surface of the curb would be a relief. "How far does the pedestrian zone extend?"

"Not far. It's confined to the lanes around the town square. Patrick Street—that's the main street through Ballybeg—allows vehicles."

They walked in silence, past flashing neon signs, pungent takeouts, and little stores with gorgeous window displays. She paused to admire one such display —traditional Irish pottery bowls, jugs, and cups. Some were decorated with glossy swirls of color; others had delicate hand painted patterns.

Ruairí's arm slipped through hers, startling her. "Planning a shopping spree?"

"I definitely want to visit this store when it's open. The pottery is gorgeous." She adjusted quickly to the familiar sensation of walking arm-in-arm with her husband.

A few feet farther down the street, they stopped before a bookstore. It was situated in a lovely turquoise building with beautiful bay windows. Spotlights lighted up a huge display of mystery novels. "Hey, I know that author." She leaned closer to get a better look. "I have a couple of his books on my ereader. They're good."

"Jonas O'Mahony is from Ballybeg."

"Really? I didn't know that. His mystery series is set in Dublin."

"Yeah, but he grew up here. He's a pal of mine. I'm sure I can persuade him to sign a book for you."

"That would be cool."

"I didn't realize you liked mysteries," he said, giving her a quizzical look. "I thought you only read literary fiction."

"I started reading mystery and romance when I was in..." *The hospital.* She stopped herself in time. This was neither the time nor the place to tell him what had happened. "Let's just say the past year was stressful. Reading genre fiction helped me unwind."

He nodded slowly, his intelligent eyes processing her every word, gesture, and intonation. "Did we move too fast, Jayme? Is that why it fell apart so easily?"

"I don't know. Six months from first date to wedding vows isn't breakneck speed."

"But it's pretty close. We were so caught up in the high of being in love. Maybe we skipped a few steps."

She drew in a shaky breath. He was right. They'd fallen for one another hard and fast, and that was how they'd conducted their entire relationship. They both had high-pressure jobs and worked long hours. What little free time they'd had, they'd spent on extravagant dates and big gestures. Had they been so busy working and making love that they'd failed to appreciate the little things? When had they spent proper downtime together? How many conversations had they postponed?

They continued their walk, Ruairí pointing out various buildings of historical importance. He was a gifted tour guide with an interesting tidbit or amusing anecdote for every place they stopped. Eventually they reached Beach Road. They stood in front of Mrs. Keogh's bed-and-breakfast, the scent of seaweed drifting up from the seashore. It reminded her of the vast expanse of water separating them from her home in New York. She shivered in the chill night air and slipped her arm free from his. "Thank you for the tour."

"My pleasure." He was staring at her intensely, his face close. Leaning in, his lips brushed her cheek. "Goodnight, Jayme. Thanks for helping me in the pub today."

Her breath caught in her throat. "No problem," she said hoarsely. "I'll see you tomorrow."

With a parting smile, he turned and retraced his steps in the direction of the town center. She watched his retreating back—so broad and strong—and caressed the cheek he'd kissed. Perhaps there was hope for them after all.

***

By the middle of her second day helping out at the pub, Jayme's feet were screaming for a massage. She stretched her stiff bones and rubbed the small of her back. When was the last time she'd been on her feet this long? Probably not since her residency at New York-Pres.

Ruairí poked his head around the kitchen door. "How's it going?"

She gave him a warm smile. "It's going."

"Can I tempt you with a coffee?"

"Coffee sounds wonderful."

"Coming right up." He hovered in the doorway. An emotion she couldn't pinpoint flickered across his face. "Want to come out to the bar for a break? It's pretty quiet at the moment. Most of the lunchtime customers have left."

"Yeah. That would be great." She untied Marcella's crazy apron—a green, white, and gold monstrosity featuring a picture of a demented-looking leprechaun drinking a pint of Guinness atop a pot of gold—and hung it on the hook by the door.

Out in the main bar, John-Joe and Buck were playing a game of cards with a couple of their drinking pals. An attractive redhead of about thirty sat at a window table, leafing through a glossy magazine. Otherwise, the pub was deserted.

"Trade will pick up again this evening," Ruairí said, reading her mind. He placed a cappuccino in front of her and handed her a teaspoon and a packet of artificial sweetener. "But Marcella will be back by then, and she can deal with the throng."

Jayme tore open the packet and stirred the sweetener into her coffee. "Any word on how her interview went?"

"Not so far."

The redhead approached the bar, clutching a gorgeous purse. It was a Gucci model Jayme had admired in Saks a few months back. The woman gave her a warm smile and extended a hand. "You must be the mysterious Mrs. MacCarthy. I'm Olivia. Welcome to Ballybeg."

Jayme blinked and accepted the handshake. "I... thank you."

"News travels fast in this town." Olivia's dark blue eyes twinkled. "Did Ruairí tell you Ballybeg literally means 'small town'? It comes from the Gaelic *baile beag*. As you've probably discovered, it more than lives up to its name."

"No, I didn't know that. The only Gaelic I know is *sláinte*."

The other woman laughed. "That's the only Gaelic you need to know around here." She slid a banknote across the bar to Ruairí. "Thanks for the lunch. I'd better get back to the office."

"Any word from Gavin and Fiona?" he asked.

"I had an e-mail from Fiona yesterday," the woman said. "Seems they're having a grand old time in Australia."

"Good to hear it."

"Say, Jayme." Olivia leaned on the counter. "If you're staying in Ballybeg for a while, maybe we can do coffee. The Book Mark Café is a good spot to meet for a scone and a chat."

"I'm not sure how long I'll be here," Jayme said, deliberately not looking in Ruairí's direction, "but if I extend my vacation, I'd love to meet up with you."

Olivia's smile widened. "Excellent. Ruairí has my number. Give me a call and we'll sort something out."

As Olivia opened the pub door to leave, Marcella marched in. She had a triumphant grin plastered across her wide face. Her black pants and shirt would have looked conservative had they not been accompanied by a multicolored top hat. A pretty woman a couple of years Marcella's junior lagged a few steps behind her. She gave Jayme a tentative smile.

"I totally rocked my interview." Marcella beamed at Jayme. "Thanks a million for filling in for me. I owe you one."

"No problem." Her delight was infectious. "It was my pleasure."

"This is Máire, my girlfriend." Marcella jerked a thumb at her shy companion.

"Pleased to meet you," Jayme said with a smile.

"To show how grateful I am for you filling in for me at such short notice, Máire's offered to help me run the pub for the next couple of days. Sharon says she's already volunteered her services on Monday. That means you two can go do touristy stuff before Jayme heads back to the States. What do you say?" Marcella looked from Jayme to her brother.

"Oh, I..." Actually, it was a fabulous idea. Sharon's forecast had proved accurate, and they were enjoying delightfully mild spring weather. She'd loved exploring Ballybeg with Ruairí yesterday evening. The prospect of seeing more of Ireland sounded fantastic.

She slid him a hopeful look. He was regarding his sister with a strange expression, some silent sibling communication passing between them. Finally he turned and met her gaze. "Would you like to see a bit of Ireland before you fly back? Beyond the daytrip we'd planned for Monday?"

His expression was hard to decipher. Did he want her to say no? Was he hoping she'd say yes? She hesitated before giving her response, hope warring with the reluctance to lay herself open to being hurt all over again.

"Of course Jayme wants to see the sights," Marcella said, nudging her brother in the ribs. If Ruairí's wince were any indication, his sister's elbow packed a punch. "And you're just the man to show her around."

"Ruairí's great on local history," Máire added. "He'll know where to take you."

Jayme caught his eye. "Are you sure? If you've got other plans..."

"No," he replied quickly. "I'd be delighted. I'll collect you from Mrs. Keogh's after breakfast tomorrow. Say about nine o'clock?"

Anticipation turned her stomach into a dance recital. She grinned at her kinda-sorta-still-husband. "That sounds perfect."

CHAPTER SEVEN

....

A t nine o'clock the following morning, Ruairí collected a bouncing Jayme from outside Mrs. Keogh's Ruairí collected a bouncing Jayme from outside Mrs. Keogh's bed-and-breakfast. She'd swapped her high heels for sensible flats and wore a bright orange windbreaker.

"I went shopping," she explained breathlessly when she slid into the passenger seat. "I didn't think my feet could cope with a day of wandering around tourist sights if I didn't buy new shoes. And I'm so over Mrs. Keogh's raincoat."

He smiled at her. "I certainly won't lose you in that ensemble."

She laughed and pulled a tourist guide from her coat pocket. "The choice in Ballybeg is *somewhat* limited. I took the only one I could find that was small enough to fit me. I drew the line at venturing into the children's department."

Ruairí flipped the indicator and pulled out into the sparse traffic. "So where would you like to go today? Has your guidebook given you any ideas?"

"Well," she said, flipping through the book thoughtfully, "we'd talked about visiting Blarney Castle. Is it far from here?"

"Not at all. It's about an hour's drive, give or take."

"Could we go there today?" Her tone was plaintive.

He laughed. "Sure. Why are you so keen on Blarney Castle?"

"It looks gorgeous in the photos. The nearest thing I've ever seen to a medieval castle was at Disney World."

Ruairí snorted with laughter. "I think we can find you something a little more authentic, but I will warn you that there's not much to see of the castle itself. It's mostly a ruin, but you can visit the dungeon, the battlements, and explore the structure."

"And it has the Blarney Stone." Jayme gave a dreamy sigh. "It sounds so romantic. I can't wait to kiss it."

Frankly, he'd far prefer she kissed him than a filthy stone. "You must be joking. That's only for tourists."

"Ruairí, I *am* a tourist."

Yes, she was... and one who was set to return to America in a few days time. His gut twisted at the thought of her leaving. Apart from skirting around the topic, they'd avoided discussing the divorce. With the date of her departure looming, they couldn't put it off much longer.

"All right," he said with a smile. "Let's find you a dirty stone to kiss. Just don't expect me to follow suit."

She teased him with her eyebrow. "Come on. Live a little. I promise I won't tell anyone in Ballybeg that one of their own deigned to kiss the Blarney Stone."

"That thing is probably diseased."

"Coward."

"I am not." He slid her a look and caught her grinning at him like the Cheshire cat. "Oh, all right. If you kiss the damn thing, I will, too. To be honest, the stone's not my favorite part of the castle. It's a great way to attract tourists, to be sure, but the legend's a crock of shite in my opinion."

"What is your favorite part of the castle?"

They'd left Ballybeg behind them now and were winding their way toward the N71. "Rock Close. It's part of the grounds of Blarney Castle. The whole area's gorgeous, but I particularly like the Blarney Dolmen."

Jayme flicked through her guidebook. "What's that?"

"A megalithic portal tomb. Great slabs of rock positioned in the shape of a door. The Celts built them all over the British Isles and beyond."

"It sounds magical."

She was magical. "It is."

"This is so exciting. I can't wait to tell my friends I saw a real castle. And kissed the Blarney Stone!"

Her enthusiasm was infectious. He recalled the same bouncing enthusiasm when they'd visited Mexico on their honeymoon. "Don't get too excited," he cautioned. "It's really not all that."

"Oh, you're only saying that because you're Irish. You take such a national treasure for granted."

He chuckled. "The stone is rumored to be a fake, you know."

"Even if it is, it's an historical fake."

"I don't follow your logic, but okay. Let's go see your historical fake."

She was examining her guidebook. "It says here the castle was built in 1446 by Dermot MacCarthy, King of Munster. Are you really descended from a king?"

He gave a bark of laughter. "Yeah... me and everyone else around here named MacCarthy. Trust me, there are quite a few of us."

Jayme flipped to the map. "Where's Munster? I don't see it on the map."

"You're *in* Munster. Historically, Ireland was divided into four provinces: Ulster in the north, Leinster to the east, Connacht to the west, and Munster to the southwest. For a time, the MacCarthy clan ruled Munster. The provinces still exist, but they have no political significance anymore."

"That's fascinating. Despite what my mother would have you believe, our ancestors hardly came over on the Mayflower. My father's family was English and my mother is a Swiss-Irish-Welsh hybrid. Neither of my parents have any interest in visiting Europe." She shook her head. "I can't understand why."

"They like sailing in hot climates," Ruairí said. "For that sort of vacation, the Caribbean is far more suitable."

"Ruairí?" Her tone was hesitant.

"Yeah?"

"I owe you an apology."

He glanced at her, noting her suddenly serious visage. "What for?"

"For not standing up for you when my parents were rude to you. I should have told them not to speak to you like that instead of making excuses for them and simply trying to keep you guys apart."

"It's okay. Really." He traced the grooves of her palm with his fingertips. "Frankly, I don't care what they think of me. I only ever cared what *you* thought of me."

"But you stood up for me to your father."

He grimaced. "To be fair, your parents' snide comments and icy disdain are a little easier to tolerate than my father's obnoxious behavior. All I can say is that it's not personal. He's like that with everyone. He's a deeply unhappy man who takes pleasure in bullying others."

She digested this a moment. "Was he in prison a lot?"

"He did two spells when I was a kid. Five years for armed robbery and another three for assault and battery."

"Wow. He was away for eight years of your childhood?"

"Yeah. I didn't miss him. Those were the happiest years. After a time, I got to hoping he'd never come back. But he always did." *Back like the proverbial bad penny.*

"Why didn't your mother leave him?"

"I don't know. I don't think she knows either. It wasn't done in her generation, and she had so many kids. By the time Sharon graduated school, Ma was sick."

"I don't ever want to feel I'm living my life for someone else, not even for my children."

"Neither do I. But you're not Ma. You're well educated and independent. You're not reliant on anyone."

Ruairí drummed the steering wheel. Was that part of their problem? Did he feel she was so self-contained that he was afraid to admit his own insecurities to her, to lay his soul bare, warts and all? Or was he just thinking of piss-poor excuses for not having tracked her down months ago and forced her to listen to him?

They passed the rest of the journey with small talk and historical vignettes. There was little traffic, and made they good time. Shortly before ten, he pulled into the car park at Blarney Castle.

Jayme, spying the castle in the distance, was in raptures. "Look at its little turrets. Aren't they darling?"

He regarded the castle's facade critically. "You'll be glad of those flat shoes by the end of today. If I recall correctly, the castle itself is around a ten-minute walk from the entrance, and it takes a couple of hours to walk around the grounds."

She slipped her hand into his. The heat from her small hand sent shock waves of awareness through his veins. He'd missed this. He'd missed her. And unless he got his act together and told her how he felt, he'd be missing her permanently. "Come on," he said, tugging her forward. "Let's go exploring."

***

Blarney Castle surpassed Jayme's expectations. As Ruairí had said, there wasn't much left of the interior, but the keep and the outer walls were still intact.

They'd ascended to the top of the castle. To reach the Blarney Stone, one had to lean backwards over the parapet. According to Jayme's guidebook, many people had died trying to kiss the stone before metal railings were fitted to break any potential falls.

Ruairí was staring at the stone with an expression of terror written across his face. "I'm not leaning back over that... precipice... and kissing a filthy stone."

"Come on, honey," she teased. "Just one little kiss."

"If I do this, it's because I'm insane or insanely in love," he muttered underneath his breath.

Jayme's heart skipped a beat. "I'm kind of hoping it's the latter."

His warm brown eyes met hers. "You know how I feel about you."

"Do I?" Their shared look lingered. She took a deep breath. "We need to talk. About us. About our future."

"I know we do. I've brought a picnic basket for our lunch, but why don't we go to a restaurant for dinner? We can enjoy our day, then talk in peace over a meal."

"Sounds good." The moment of tension passed. "But you're not getting out of kissing that stone."

He groaned. "You're relentless."

She grinned at him. "Tell you what. You kiss the stone now, and later, I'll kiss you. Deal?"

Sexual awareness flared in his dark eyes. His gaze trailed down her body, then back to her face. The corners of his mouth twitched. "You drive a hard bargain Dr. King."

When he leaned back, his shirt inched upward, revealing a tantalizing glimpse of rock hard abs. Her pulse quickened. His lips touched the stone for the briefest second, before he pulled himself back into a sitting position. "Ugh. That was gross."

"Chicken," she said, laughing. "Your lips barely touched it."

He shuddered. "The barest contact was sufficient to confirm my suspicion that the stone is disease-ridden."

He stood, yanking his shirt back into place. A shame. She'd missed seeing that taut stomach.

"Want to explore the grounds?" He extended his arm, and she slipped her hand back into his.

"Sure," she said. "I want to see that dolmen you mentioned."

He led her down stone steps and through the ruined courtyard toward the gardens. The guidebook hadn't done them justice. They were gorgeous, several little sections just beginning to bloom. Jayme peered at one of the plants. "What a beautiful flower." She leaned closer. "What a sec... that almost looks like—"

"Wolfsbane," Ruairí said, pointing to the sign.

"Aconite?" She drew back in alarm. "Wow. They weren't joking when they named this part of the grounds Poison Garden."

"No, they weren't. Hey, if you want to save money on the divorce, mandrake's over there." His teasing smile warmed her in spite of the February chill.

She quirked an eyebrow, wavering between annoyance and amusement that he could joke about their marital issues. "I'm a doctor. If I was planning to kill you, I'm pretty sure I could come up with a more subtle poison than mandrake."

Her tone must have tipped him off that he'd irritated her. He frowned, then said: "I'm sorry, Jayme. It slipped out."

"Lead me toward this famous portal tomb and I might forgive you."

"We're nearly there. Rock Close is up ahead."

They wandered through the rest of the gardens, eventually reaching the area Ruairí had pointed to.

"Seeing as we kissed the stone," he said, "we'd better continue our day of superstitions and descend the Wishing Steps backward."

"The Wishing Steps? How charming."

"There's a catch, though."

She laughed. "Isn't there always?"

"You have to do it with your eyes shut."

"In other words, if we manage to get down the steps without falling and breaking our necks, all our wishes will come true?"

He flashed her a wolfish grin. "That's about the size of it."

"Come on then. Let's do it."

"You have to think of a wish first, but don't tell me."

Her wish didn't require a second's consideration. Rewinding the clock and changing the choices they'd made a year ago wasn't feasible, but if the past few days were any indication, rekindling their marriage was still within the realm of the possible. She squeezed her eyes shut. "I'm ready."

He took her hand in his and they slowly maneuvered themselves down the steps.

"Oh," she said, losing her footing. His strong arm broke her fall. Finally, after a couple more near misses, they made it to the bottom of the steps intact.

She sagged against the wall, laughing. "So what did you wish for?"

He smiled. "It's bad luck to tell you. You going to tell me your wish?"

"I'm superstitious enough not to want to tempt fate." Their eyes met and time froze.

"Jayme." His voice was hoarse and thick with longing. He leaned forward and brushed her lips with his. His mouth parted, revealing very white, very even teeth. Her breath caught when he leaned in again. This time, she matched him movement for movement, their tongues meshing in an erotic dance. She slipped her hands inside his jacket, kneading the taut muscles beneath his shirt.

"Jayme." He murmured her name again against her ear. Every hair on her nape stood to attention. One of his hands slipped under her windbreaker. The sensation of him touching her burned through her thin wool sweater. He ran the other hand through her hair, loosening it from its ribbon. It cascaded over her shoulders and down her back.

"Your hair's longer," he said, examining it.

"Do you like it?"

"Yeah. Definitely. The longer style suits you." He let the strands fall through his fingers. "It's beautiful. You're beautiful."

Her cheeks grew warm. "You're a shameless flatterer, Ruairí MacCarthy."

"No flattery needed. It's the truth." He buried his face in her hair, and the smell of his spicy aftershave sent her hormones into overdrive. "I've missed you, Jayme. So very much."

"You can't possibly have missed me as much as I've missed you." Her voice broke on the words. She'd have to tell him the truth about why she hadn't returned his calls. As much as she wanted to bury it in the past, he'd have to know before they could move forward.

His eyes were clouded with emotion. "I can live a reasonably contented life without you in it, Jayme, but something's always missing. It's like a big gaping wound that never heals."

She was shaking with nerves, breathless with anticipation. She leaned into him, smelled the detergent from his shirt. "I was barely going through the motions in New York. I want you back in my life. I don't know how we'll swing it, but I want to try."

He cupped her chin in his palm. "I booked us a hotel nearby. I didn't say it before because I didn't want to put you under any pressure. At the very least, they have a great restaurant if we want to have dinner there."

Her breathing labored, she pulled his head toward her and nibbled his earlobe. "The only dinner I'll be interested in will come via room service."

....

CHAPTER EIGHT

The hotel Ruairí had booked was perfect. It reminded Jayme of a manor house in one her favorite Masterpiece Theater series, complete with a four-poster bed.

But while she would normally be enraptured by the hotel's architecture and decor, all she was interested in right now was getting Ruairí naked.

"It's been so long," she murmured, burying her face into his chest and inhaling his clean, male scent. "I've probably forgotten how to do it."

"I doubt that. I haven't slept with anyone since you, and my body definitely hasn't forgotten what to do." He ran his fingers through her hair, then trailed kisses down her neck, making her gasp in anticipation.

She steeled herself to ask the question that had been nagging her since her arrival in Ballybeg. "Marcella mentioned you were seeing someone named Laura."

"We hadn't gotten as far as our first date, never mind sex." His lips continued their torturous trail. "When you showed up, I canceled. You're the woman I want."

The coil of tension in her stomach eased. Had he dated someone in the past year, she couldn't have held it against him, but it was a relief to know he hadn't. His fingers roamed over her arms. She gasped at his touch, her skin turning electric. He'd always had the power to turn her on, even after the most colossal row. Their sexual connection had been a major part in their relationship. How important hadn't become clear until the night he'd left and she'd realized how little she knew about the man she'd married.

He undid the buttons of her shirt and shoved the material off her shoulders to reveal bare skin. When he toyed with her bra strap and teased the skin underneath with his fingertips, her nipples pebbled.

"Ruairí." She'd have to tell him before he saw her naked. "There's something—"

"Shh." He put a finger to her lips. "Not a word."

In one fluid movement, he undid the clasp of her bra and it fell to the floor.

Taking a deep breath, she eased her panties down her hips and past the pale pink slash across her abdomen.

He registered the scar immediately. "What's this?" His fingers hovered above the start of the neat scar, still tender even after all these months.

"That's what I was trying to tell you." The words tumbled out in a breathless rush.

"What happened to you?" His eyes searched hers. "This can't be an appendix scar. It's on your left side."

"No, it wasn't my appendix." She swallowed past the lump in her throat. "I had to have a fallopian tube removed."

Shock turned his face rigid. "My god." His hands steadied on her shoulders. "Why?"

Now for the fun bit, the part she'd been avoiding. "I had an ectopic pregnancy."

His face underwent a series of contortions. "You were pregnant?"

She nodded. She could see the wheels in his mind at work, calculating dates. "When did this happen?"

"A few weeks after you flew to Ireland. I must have been in the early stages of pregnancy when you left."

His face crumpled into an expression of utter devastation. "Oh, no. Jayme. I am so, so sorry. Why didn't you tell me? I'd have come over on the next flight."

"I know. That's *why* I didn't tell you. I needed time to think. I was in shock. I hadn't known I was pregnant. My periods were always light. When I had one that was even lighter than normal, I didn't think anything was amiss. It wasn't until the pain started that I realized something was very wrong. Even then, I assumed it was a stomach problem—an ulcer or something similar. When the ER doctor told me I was pregnant, I was stunned. Physicians make the worst patients, and we're usually lousy at diagnosing ourselves."

His voice broke when he spoke. "There was nothing they could do to save the baby?"

She shook her head. "An ectopic pregnancy isn't viable."

"Will you be able—" He stopped himself. "I'm sorry. I don't want to upset you."

"The answer to that is... I don't know. I'm down one fallopian tube, and I had an infection afterward." A tear slid down her cheek, and she brushed it away. "I might not be able to conceive naturally."

"Oh, sweetheart." He hugged her close. His tender touch was too much for her fragile self-control. She began to cry in earnest, big fat tears and proper sobs. "Shh," he whispered. "Let it all out."

"After... after it happened, I bottled it up. I was numb. I forced myself not to think about it for months. I went back to work and went through the motions, ignoring my tendency to self-medicate with wine as soon as I got home. Then one day, I broke down. My parents checked me into a clinic for a few weeks to recover."

"I should have been there for you. Why don't you hate me for not being there?"

"I don't hate you because I didn't tell you. I *chose* not to tell you. I'm sorry if this sounds cruel, but I don't regret it. I think I needed that time alone. It allowed me to concentrate on my own grief without worrying about how you were coping. Of course, if I'd known about your mother, I'd have gotten in touch with you ages ago."

"And if I'd known—" He shook his head. "We could go round in circles with this, couldn't we?" He stroked her cheek tenderly.

"Perhaps it would be easier if I did hate you. I don't know. What happened with... with the baby... wasn't your fault. We're both to blame for the fight that split us up. Yes, you should have told me the truth about your family, but perhaps you were right. Maybe I wouldn't have listened. Maybe I would have reacted like a snob if I knew your dad and brother had done time. I don't know. Frankly, I don't want to know."

"It doesn't matter, Jayme." His deep voice broke with emotion. "You're here now, and we're talking. I should have trusted you. I should have told you the whole story —every goddamn sordid detail. You deserved to know the background of the man you were about to marry."

She buried her face into his chest, inhaled his spicy scent. "Make love to me, Ruairí."

"Are you sure you want to?" He stroked her hair, making her shiver with anticipation. "We could just cuddle if you'd prefer."

"No, I need you to make love to me. I want to feel like a woman again, not a sexless, potentially infertile shell. I'm not looking to try to get pregnant. I want to... feel. It's like I've been numb for months."

"Okay." He stroked her upper thighs, kneading the precise points he knew she was the most sensitive. "If you want to stop at any point, tell me."

"I won't want to stop." She tugged at his shirt. "This. Off."

His fingers flew over the buttons, but every second was one too long for her. She slipped her hands under his shirt, massaging his skin, pulling at his nipples.

"Feck." He gave the buttons up as a lost cause and pulled his shirt over his head.

Hers fingers wandered to his belt. When she brushed against his groin, he groaned. "I want you so much, Jayme. I feel like I'm going to explode."

"I sincerely hope you do. Just hold off for a few minutes, okay?"

She undid his jeans, one button at a time. He gasped when she stroked his hardness, straining against the confines of his underwear.

She nibbled his lip. His breath came in staccato gasps.

When she pulled his jeans down over his hips, he wriggled himself free from his underpants.

"Wow." She ran a fingertip down his silky length, careful not to graze him with her sharp nail. She sank to her knees and teased the tip with her tongue, registered his sharp intake of breath. She grew more adventurous, slowly wandering down his stiff shaft, feeling the smooth skin against her tongue. He tasted salty, masculine. She drew her tongue back up in slow, circular movements.

"Jayme," he gasped. "You're torturing me."

"Hmm?" She pulsated her tongue around the tip of his erection, making him groan with pleasure.

"I want you on your back," he growled.

"What are you going to do to get me there?" she teased.

"You'll find out." In one fluid movement, he flipped her onto her back, strategically aiming her head for the pillow. She laughed out loud. It was a trick he'd perfected on their honeymoon when she'd complained she always landed between both pillows rather than on one.

He stroked her inner thighs again, each movement sending volts of pleasure skittering across her skin. She shoved his hand higher, positioning him directly between her legs. He stroked her clit, slowly at first, in long, drawn-out circular movements.

She gave a moue of impatience and applied pressure to his hand until he hit the right tempo. "Ah," she sighed. "So good."

A few minutes later, he flipped her on her front and pulled her into a kneeling position.

"What?" she teased. "You cruel man."

"I did tell you," he whispered into her ear, "that I'd stop anytime you wanted me to. You asking me to stop?"

His erection teased her entrance, making her gasp.

"Hell, no. If you stop now, I'll get my revenge."

His laughter reverberated against her ear. "In that case..."

One thrust later, he was inside her. He gave her a moment to grow accustomed to his size, and then began to move. As if on cue, her hips met him thrust for thrust, each more exhilarating than its predecessor.

The pressure inside her built to a crescendo until she was shook by a tsunami of pleasure.

She was still getting her breath back when she felt him come.

Afterward, they collapsed onto their pillows, spent and exhausted.

"That was... amazing," she said through a yawn. And then blissful sleep enveloped her.

***

The next morning, Ruairí woke to find Jayme propped up on her pillow, staring at him. The sight of her flushed face and sleep-tousled hair warmed him to the core.

"I'm still in love with you, Ruairí," she blurted, and then turned even redder.

He stroked her cheek, marveling at the softness of her skin. "And I'm still in love with you."

"So what are we going to do?" One breast peeked out from beneath the sheet. "Is your heart set on staying in Ireland?"

"The only thing my heart is set on is staying with you. Would you consider living in Ireland for a few months? If you didn't like it, we'd go back to New York."

Her brow creased. "I've thought about my possibilities. I could look for someone to cover my job for a few months. I'm reluctant to sell my share of the practice until we're more certain where we want to live long-term."

"I understand. If I had a few months to finish overseeing the renovations, I could hire a manager to run the pub for me and go back to the States with you."

She touched his jaw, tickling his stubble. "You should spend your mother's last days with her. I'd never ask you to give up that chance. I'll have to return to New York in

85

a few days to sort out a locum and someone to look after the apartment. Once that's taken care of, I'll be on the next flight back to Ireland."

He let out the breath he hadn't noticed he'd been holding. Hearing her say she wanted to be with him was an enormous relief. He'd been dreading her return to New York. He was still dreading it, but at least he now knew she'd be coming back. "Are you sure you can bear to live here for a few months? It's nothing like what you're used to."

"No, and that's why I like it. But its main selling point is you." She leaned forward and kissed him on the chin. "The real question is whether or not you can bear the thought of living in New York again."

Their fingers entwined, and he brought her knuckles to his lips. "Honestly? I don't know. If you wanted to go back, I'd go with you."

"But you said you were sick of the rat race of Wall Street and happy here in Ballybeg."

"I said I was *content*. Your absence left a gaping hole. As long as I'm with you, I don't care where we live. Whether we make our home in Manhattan or Ballybeg is something we can decide later. The most important thing is to decide we want to be together, regardless of location."

"I definitely want to be with you," she said, squeezing his shoulder. "But I want you to be happy."

"If I move back to New York, I doubt I'll go back to being a stockbroker." He looked her straight in the eye.

"Could you live with me bringing home less money than I used to earn?"

"Of course." She didn't hesitate before answering. "If there's one thing the past year has proved, it's that material things don't mean a damn if you've no one to share them with. If you find a job that makes you happy, we'll find a solution."

He caught her up in his arms and kissed her hard. "I love you, Jayme King. So damn much. I want to make our marriage work."

"So do I. I'm willing to give it a few months to decide where we want to live." She nuzzled his ear. "But there's one condition."

"And what's that?" he asked, teasing the cleft in her chin.

She fingered the indent on his wedding finger. "We're getting you a new ring."

EPILOGUE

....

SEVEN MONTHS LATER

The weekend after Molly's funeral, Jayme and Ruairí packed a picnic and drove out to Mizen Head. drove out to Mizen Head. A wet August had given way to a blissfully sunny September. The leaves on the trees were showing the first signs of fall, and the busy tourist season that had kept them busy in the pub was starting to ebb.

Jayme had surprised herself by how much she'd enjoyed spending the last few months in Ireland. Their living quarters over the pub were cramped, and the constant awareness of Molly's illness was stressful. However, she'd cherished the opportunity to get to know her mother-in-law before she died. She'd never warm to her father-in-law, but she liked most of Ruairí's siblings, especially Sharon and Marcella.

And as for Ruairí himself... she lowered her binoculars and eyed her handsome husband with appreciation while he set out their picnic. Reconnecting with him had been a wonderful experience. They'd talked more over the past few months than they had during the three years they were together in New York. At times, it had been painful, but the newfound emotional trust between them more than made up for her discomfort discussing the aftermath of her surgery.

He caught her watching him and grinned. "Didn't I tell you the view up here was good?"

She placed the binoculars on the blanket. "Good? Honey, it's spectacular."

He shaded his eyes against the low September sun. "Funny to think our apartment in Manhattan is all the way across the ocean."

She stared out at the crashing waves below the cliffs and at the vast expanse of ocean beyond. "Funny to think I don't miss it. Who would have thought I'd enjoy living in a small Irish town?"

Ruairí flipped open the picnic basket and extracted a bottle and two champagne flutes. He popped the cork and poured a generous amount of bubbly liquid into each glass.

"No, I can't," she said when he handed her one.

Amusement creased his eyes. "Am I to continue ignoring your sudden reluctance to drink alcohol, or are you finally ready to tell me why?"

She laughed. "I like to keep you in suspense."

"Does it have anything to do with what you told Ma just before she died? Whatever it was, it certainly put a smile on her face."

Jayme placed her champagne flute on top of picnic basket. Her fingers trembled slightly. "It might." She took a deep breath. "As of today, I'm twelve weeks pregnant."

His face split into a wide grin. "I knew it! Sweetheart, that's the best news I've heard since... well, forever." He moved to her side of the blanket and caught her up into a kiss.

"I wanted to wait until I was past the first trimester," she said, leaning into his chest. "I'd have told you no matter what happened, but I couldn't let myself think about it until then, you know?"

He stroked her cheek. "But you told Ma."

"Yeah." She glanced up. "You don't mind?"

He kissed her tenderly on the forehead. "Not at all. I wish she'd lived long enough to see our baby born, but I'm glad she had the chance to know he or she was on the way. Thank you for giving her that gift."

"Seeing as we're talking babies, I'd better tell you I've been offered a part-time position at a pediatric clinic in Cork City."

"Seriously?" Hope flickered across his face. "Did you accept?"

"Yes. I can't guarantee I'll want to live in Ireland forever, but we're happy here at the moment. I'm more than willing to give it a chance."

He drew her into his arms. "I love you, Jayme King."

"And I love you, Ruairí MacCarthy." She patted her still-flat abdomen. "But I think it's time we searched for a house."

"In Ballybeg?" he asked, his expression hopeful.

She smiled. "Where else?"

THANK YOU!

....

Thanks for reading *Love and Blarney*. I hope you enjoyed it! *Love and Blarney* is the second book in the Ballybeg series. All the stories are designed to stand alone—Happy Ever Afters guaranteed! However, you might prefer to read them in order of publication to follow the development of the secondary characters and happenings in the town.

To find out what's next, or to sign up to my new release mailing list, check out my author website at:

http://zarakeane.com

You can also turn the page to read blurbs for *Love and Shenanigans* (Ballybeg, #1) and *Love and Leprechauns* (Ballybeg, #3).

LOVE AND LEPRECHAUNS

(BALLYBEG, #3)

....

Tattooed in Tipperary...
Olivia Gant is determined to escape her abusive husband and build a new life. Only desperation drives her to rent business premises from Jonas O'Mahony, the man who tattooed her behind and broke her heart. Can she maintain a haughty distance?

Jonas is a struggling single father. The last person he wants next door is the beautiful-but-infuriating Olivia. A childcare crisis forces him to strike a bargain with her: the lease to the cottage in return for babysitting. Can he resist her allures?

...True Love in Ballybeg.
When Olivia's ex is clobbered to death by a garden gnome, the fickle finger of suspicion points to Olivia and Jonas. Can they prove their innocence, or is their happily ever after doomed?

**OUT NOW! TURN THE PAGE
FOR AN EXCERPT.**

EXCERPT FROM

LOVE AND LEPRECHAUNS

....

BALLYBEG, COUNTY CORK, IRELAND

The door to the dental office swung open, bringing in a gust of wind and Jonas O'Mahony. Olivia staggered back. A strong arm grabbed her wrist, breaking her fall. His fingers sent heat searing through the layers of clothing. Blood hummed in her veins. She blamed the Novocain. Breathing hard, she yanked her arm free.

For years, she'd managed to avoid him. Easy enough to do—he didn't exactly run in the same circles as Aidan. Since his best friend had hooked up with hers, they'd crossed paths more frequently than she liked.

"Olivia." His gravelly voice broke the silence, as deep and rough as single-cask whiskey.

"Jonath," she lisped. *Silly anesthetic.*

He gave her a cool once-over, his indifferent expression indicating he wasn't impressed with what he saw.

She returned the favor. Jonas's broad frame was encased in leather and biker boots. His overly long black

93

hair had a wild look that she suspected was caused by the recent removal of a motorcycle helmet. His dark eyes riveted her in place. She sensed the leprechaun on her behind burning a hole through her skirt. What had possessed her to commemorate her eighteenth birthday by getting a leprechaun tattooed on her arse? Her erratic heart thumped an extra beat. She knew the answer to that question. It wasn't *what* but *who,* and she was looking right at him.

"Jonas," Julie cooed from the reception desk. "How are you? How's your adorable little boy? Luca, isn't it?"

Blech. Clearly, Julie laid on more than makeup with a trowel.

"Hey, Julie." He treated the receptionist to a warm smile—treacle hot and sickly sweet. "Luca's grand. Adjusting to his new environment, but he'll get there. Should I take a seat in the waiting room?"

The receptionist's face registered disappointment that her flirting had failed to have the desired effect. "There are a few people ahead of you. You might have to wait for a bit."

"No problem." Jonas strode past Olivia without sparing her another glance. She caught a whiff of his aftershave—spicy and exotic. It sent her whirling back in time to the heady days of their love affair—intense, passionate, cut short by tragedy.

The vibration of her phone jolted her back to the present. *Shite.* Why was she still at the dentist? She needed to get moving. Holding the phone to her ear, she pushed open the door and stepped out into the blustery gale. She'd have to talk while she walked, and she'd better do both fast.

"This is Mary McDermott..." The woman's voice trailed off in an ominous ellipsis.

Not a positive sign. Please let this not be bad news about her bid for the cottage. "Yeah?"

"I'm afraid circumstances have changed. The cottages on Curzon Street are no longer available to rent. I'm sorry."

Sorry? The hell she is. Olivia was temporarily bereft of speech. "We had an agreement," she said finally, forcing herself to remain calm. Now was not the time to lose her cool. "You said I could have one of the vacant cottages if I paid the deposit by the end of the month. It's only the sixteenth." Courtesy of the anesthetic-induced lisp, each "s" came out as "th".

"We discussed you renting one of my properties, but we never got around to signing a contract." Mary's tone was defensive, bordering on peevish.

"I emailed you a reminder about the contract last week. You never replied."

"A landlady needs to know her prospective tenant will pay the rent on time and stay longer than a handful of months."

Whoa... that was way out of line. "Which prospective tenant proved solvent enough to get more than an oral agreement out of you?"

"You know I can't reveal that information. It's confidential."

"As was *my* bid for the bigger cottage. That didn't stop you from telling half the town. I'll ask you again: who?"

Mary's hesitation echoed down the phone. "He's not a tenant, exactly. My nephew—"

"Not Jonath?" Olivia stumbled to a halt, her head whipping round in the direction of the dental practice. But who else could it be? Niall O'Mahony was away at university, and he and Jonas were Mary's only living nephews.

"Jonas is a good lad. When he moved back to Ballybeg with his son, he had trouble finding a place to live. Curzon Street was the obvious solution."

"Surely he doesn't need *both* cottages. Why can't I have the other?"

"You know the answer to that question." Olivia could visualize Mary's Gallic shrug. "If you want to negotiate a deal with him, go for it. He's responsible for renting out the second cottage and he's unlikely to want to live next door to you. I'm sorry, but you'll have to look for somewhere else to open your café."

She began to formulate a cutting response, but Mary had already hung up, leaving her staring at the phone clutched in her hand. *Unbelievable.* Had Jonas engineered this reversal in her fortunes? Did he hate her that much after all these years? She wasn't having it. Pivoting on her heel, she stalked to the dental practice and barged in the door.

"Something wrong?" Julie batted her false eyelashes.

Olivia ignored her and marched straight through the reception area and into the waiting room. Three heads swiveled, but she was only interested in one. She directed the full force of her glare on Jonas. "You thcheming thcumbag."

Jonas regarded her coolly. "Had a filling?" His deep voice dripped condescension.

Olivia uttered an oath.

He laughed.

The rat bastard.

"What have I done to warrant being called a 'thchumbag'?"

His exaggerated air quotes made the other waiting room occupants snigger. Olivia itched to wipe the smug expression off his face.

"You knew I wanted one of the cottages for my café. Mary and I had a deal. You played the family card and poached it from me."

"Indeed?" His expression was inscrutable. "All's fair in love, war, and business, right? There'll be other premises. It simply wasn't meant to be."

"Could you be any more patronizing?"

He gave a slow grin. "I'm sure I could if I cared enough to try."

Olivia bit her lip in frustration, then registered the acrid taste of blood. *Fantastic.* Now she was going to arrive at the bank sporting a split lip, a lisp, and no prospective business premises. Perhaps it was time to change tack and use her feminine wiles to persuade Jonas to do the right thing. The notion galled her, but that simpering crap worked for other women, didn't it?

"Jonath," she began in what she hoped was a husky tone. "I'd planned my grand opening for the beginning of June. I'll never find alternative premises in time."

His lips twitched. "Wasn't planning your 'grand opening' before you'd inked the deal premature?"

So much for her feminine wiles. Her fingernails bit into her palms. "You're despicable. I pity your son being stuck with you as his lone parent." She regretted the words the moment she uttered them. *Drat.* She should have left the kid out of this, but it was too late to backtrack now.

Jonas's eyes narrowed, his expression turning to granite.

She refused to be intimidated. She held his icy stare.

"Suck it up, Olivia," he said in glacial tones. "The cottages are mine. Find another place to open your café."

She cast him a look of loathing and stormed out of the waiting room.

"Best of luck with your search," Jonas called after her retreating form.

Ignoring Julie's gleeful expression, Olivia shoved open the front door and marched out into the gale force wind.

She was blown down Patrick Street. Ballybeg was famous for its brightly colored buildings, but the cheery facades were an insult to Olivia's black mood.

Jonas had done this deliberately. She'd known he disliked her, but sabotaging her plans for the café seemed extreme. That cottage was *hers*. She'd spent months planning the layout, knew exactly what would be positioned where. To come so close and have her dreams implode... Screw Mary McDermott and her shameless display of nepotism. And screw Jonas O'Mahony and his arrogance. *May he be struck down with an incurable case of crotch crabs.*

OUT NOW!

LOVE AND SHENANIGANS

(BALLYBEG, #1)

....

Vows in Vegas...
Three days before leaving Ireland on the adventure of a
lifetime, Fiona Byrne returns to her small Irish
hometown to attend the family wedding from hell.
When she discovers the drunken vows she exchanged
with the groom during a wild Las Vegas trip eight years
previously mean they're legally married, her future plans
ricochet out of control. Can she untangle herself from
the man who broke her heart so long ago? Does she
even want to?

...True Love in Ballybeg.
Gavin Maguire's life is low on drama, high on stability,
and free of pets. But Gavin hadn't reckoned on Fiona
blasting back into his life and crashing his wedding. In
the space of twenty-four hours, he loses a fiancée and a
job, and gains a wife and a labradoodle. Can he salvage
his bland-but-stable life? More importantly, can he resist
losing his heart to Fiona all over again?

OUT NOW!

OTHER BOOKS BY ZARA

....

1. *Love and Shenanigans* (novel)
2. *Love and Blarney* (novella)
3. *Love and Leprechauns* (novel)
4. *Love and Mistletoe* (novella)
5. *Love and Shamrocks* (novel) Coming 2015

ACKNOWLEDGEMENTS

....

Once again, I'm indebted to a number of people for their assisstance while I was preparing *Love and Blarney* for publication. Many thanks are due to my wonderful critique partner, Magdalen Braden, for her insightful suggestions on how an American might perceive rural Ireland; to Rhonda Helms, editor extraordinaire, for showing me how to focus on the romantic arc and maximize the emotional impact within the confines of a smaller word count; to Trish Slattery and Michele Harvey for beta reading the novella; and to Anne and Linda at Victory Editing for the thorough proofread.

Last but definitely not least, thank you to my family for tolerating my crazy work schedule over the past year with *mostly* good grace!

ABOUT ZARA KEANE

....

Zara Keane grew up in Dublin, Ireland, but spent her summers in a small town very similar to the fictitious Ballybeg.

She currently lives in Switzerland with her family. When she's not writing or wrestling small people, she drinks far too much coffee, and tries—with occasional success —to resist the siren call of Swiss chocolate.

zarakeane.com

28011959R00059

Printed in Great Britain
by Amazon